Laura Ingalls Is Ruining My Life

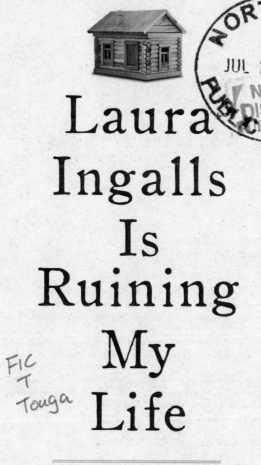

Laura Ingalls Is Ruining My Life

SHELLEY TOUGAS

SQUARE
FISH

ROARING BROOK PRESS · NEW YORK

SQUARE
FISH

An imprint of Macmillan Publishing Group, LLC
175 Fifth Avenue, New York, NY 10010
mackids.com

Square Fish and the Square Fish logo are trademarks of Macmillan and
are used by Roaring Brook Press under license from Macmillan.

Our books may be purchased in bulk for promotional, educational, or business
use. Please contact your local bookseller or the Macmillan Corporate and
Premium Sales Department at (800) 221-7945 ext. 5442 or by email
at MacmillanSpecialMarkets@macmillan.com.

Library of Congress Control Number: 2017933826

ISBN 978-1-250-30877-1 (paperback)   ISBN 978-1-62672-419-8 (ebook)

Originally published in the United States by Roaring Brook Press
First Square Fish edition, 2019
Book designed by Elizabeth Clark
Square Fish logo designed by Filomena Tuosto

10 9 8 7 6 5 4 3 2 1

AR: 4.1 / LEXILE: HL580L

For the kids who ventured west with me:
Brandon, Joshua, Brittany, and Samantha,
and for Nathan, the boy who will go next time.

· PART ONE ·

Little Basement on the Prairie

· CHAPTER ·
ONE

The highway stretched as far as you could see, but Mom insisted on stopping at the Prairie Diner.

It didn't matter that the diner looked like an abandoned shed, that only four cars sat in the parking lot, that a vent belched smoke from a deep fryer. It didn't matter because a few miles back a billboard proclaimed, AT THE PRAIRIE DINER KIDS EAT FREE ON WEDNESDAYS! It was Wednesday. There were three kids in the car. No calculator required.

"We're only twenty miles from the new place," I said. "Can't we eat when we get there? Or go to McDonald's?"

Cornfields and prairie grasses surrounded the diner. It was the only building I could see on the highway, and I could see for miles. The land was so flat a ball wouldn't roll without a hard kick.

Mom got out of the car and snapped a photo of the place with her phone. She liked to document adventures, and in her mind, a roadside diner equaled adventure. "It's perfect. Who wants to eat at a chain restaurant? There's no adventure in that."

See?

"At least it's not gas station pizza," my half sister, Rose, said.

"That's my girl." Mom smiled.

My brother, Freddy, reached into the glove compartment and pulled out a roll of duct tape. Mom said, "Freddy, do you have to do this? You're projecting negative energy, and it's not fair to the other customers." Freddy ripped a piece of tape from the roll and pressed it over his mouth. I hid a smile. "Really?" Mom asked.

Freddy nodded and walked across the gravel parking lot with Rose skipping behind him. Mom turned to me and said, "Please don't play along. I'm serious about energy. We get what we give. It's karma."

"What goes around comes around," Rose singsonged.

But by covering his mouth and staging a silent protest Freddy was doing exactly what Mom and Rose said. He was making sure "it" came back around—"it" being the bad feelings about moving from Lexington, Kentucky, to the western edge of Minnesota. We moved all the time, but always to real cities with malls and movie theaters and bus lines; never to a place like this, a land so quiet and empty the wind had nothing to blow. Rose was no help. She hadn't wanted to leave Lexington, either, but she never complained. Mom and Rose were all sunshine, all the time, the Florida of moods.

Inside a sign said SEAT YOURSELF, so Freddy picked a table in the middle of the diner. About ten people were scattered at tables, and one by one, they looked up from their meals and stared at us—at Freddy, the boy with tape on his mouth. Normally Freddy blended into the background like a beige chair against a beige wall. He kept his head low, his eyes down, his voice quiet. When you constantly switch schools, you learn to become invisible. Calling attention to yourself is an invitation to bullies. I learned that the hard way at Sherwood Elementary.

Or was it Sherman Elementary? I can never remember.

During sharing time in kindergarten, I stood up and shared that my mom could play both piano and guitar. Except I said *guiptar*. I don't know why. It just came out wrong. Everyone laughed, even though the teacher shushed them, and Tommy Jackson called me "stupid head." All week, Tommy Jackson yelled "guiptar stupid head" in my face every morning.

Was his name Tommy or Timmy?

Doesn't really matter. My point: if you don't stand up and share, nobody will call you guiptar stupid head.

I scanned the menu. "I told you, Mom. The kids menu is for kids ten and younger. Even Rose doesn't qualify for a free meal."

"Rose just turned eleven, which is practically ten. You and Freddy can pass. It'll save a ton of money." Mom ignored karma whenever it involved money.

I groaned. "This is so embarrassing."

"People shouldn't make a profit from food," Mom said. "It's an essential human need. Besides, it's not more embarrassing than your brother's vow of silence."

Freddy's cheeks lifted a bit, like he might be giving me a mission-accomplished smile through the tape. He'd taken the vow when Mom had announced she was quitting her job and moving us to a town no bigger than a pea, all so she could write her children's novel. The vow symbolized his protest about not having a voice in the decision. That's what he wrote in the tiny notebook he carried in his back pocket.

"Hot enough for you folks?" The waitress's name tag said Gloria. She held a tray across her thick belly.

"I love this weather," Mom said. "In the South this would be considered mildly warm."

"I'll take your word for it. What can I get you?"

"I'd like the grilled cheese and fries, and the kids will be ordering from the kids menu because they're nine and ten and ten." Mom pointed at me, then Freddy. "Twins."

"Sure they are." Gloria's voice was as flat as the prairie.

The part about being twins was true, but we were twelve, and we looked it.

I ordered a chicken strip basket. Freddy pointed at the menu. Gloria looked at the tape on Freddy's face and then turned to Mom, who said, "It's a silent protest. I'm trying to validate his feelings without encouraging his behavior."

Gloria raised an eyebrow and grunted. Rose asked, "What is tater tot hot dish?"

"I guess you're not from around here." I couldn't tell if Gloria thought that was a bad thing or a good thing. "It's ground beef, cream of mushroom soup, corn, green beans, and tater tots. Kids always love it."

"Sounds like an adventure. I'll try it," Rose said.

"That's my girl," Mom said.

When Gloria left, Rose said to Freddy, "Are you really going to be silent for an entire school year? Give it a chance. We might like it. We might love it."

"Freddy wants you to know he has the right to feel however he feels," I said. I knew what he was thinking because I could read him, and he could read me. We had Twin Superpowers. Freddy nodded.

Mom's eyes moved to Freddy, then to me, even though she was speaking to Rose. "I'm so proud of your positive attitude and sense of adventure. You just jump into life and enjoy it, no matter what."

When Mom praised Rose, there was always a hidden

message, and you didn't need police training to decode it. Her words said *Rose is awesome*, but she meant *Be more like Rose*. Freddy and I weren't like Rose, and we didn't want to be like Rose, sweet as a jellybean wrapped in taffy. When it rained, we saw puddles and gray sky. Rose saw the birth of a rainbow. Maybe it was because Freddy and I were older, or maybe it was because we had a different father than Rose. But Freddy and I are close. It's just the nature of twins. There's only room for two.

Rose pulled a book from her bag—*On the Banks of Plum Creek* by Laura Ingalls Wilder. "I can read out loud while we wait for our food."

"Great idea!" Mom looked at me. "Isn't it great?"

"Doesn't matter to me." Realistically, I was stuck with Laura for a year. I had to deal with her the way you deal with an upset stomach. You wait it out. Eventually you puke and feel better. Freddy had an opinion, though. His eyes widened, and he made sure we were watching as he lifted his arms, put one hand on each ear, and turned off his hearing aids.

"Nice job, Rose," I said. "Now Freddy can't speak or hear."

"That's his choice," Mom said.

"His choice." Rose cleared her throat and began reading. "Chapter one. 'The dim wagon track went no farther on the prairie, and Pa stopped the horses.'"

Gloria delivered our drinks before Rose could start the second sentence. Gloria looked at the book and smiled. "I'm a big Laura fan, too. The biggest. If you like *On the Banks of Plum Creek*, you're near the heart of it all."

"I know," Rose said. "Laura Ingalls lived here in the olden days during the grasshopper plague. That's why we're here."

"Not because of grasshoppers." Mom laughed. "We're moving to Walnut Grove because of Laura. I'm a writer."

"You're writing a book about Laura Ingalls?"

I needed to shut this down before Mom launched her crazy spirit-of-Laura explanation. "When is our food going to be ready?"

Obviously Gloria believed children should be seen and not heard because she didn't answer my question. She said, "I live a stone's throw from Walnut Grove. You'll like it. It's a nice little town. People are friendly but not too friendly, if you know what I mean. Where are you living?"

Mom said, "We're only going to be here for the school year, so we're renting. Do you know Miguel and Mia Ramos? We'll be living in their basement."

"You bet. They both work at Schwann's up in Marshall. Their granddaughter Julia just moved in with them. Seems like a sweet girl. I don't like gossip, so let's just say Julia's parents are a train wreck. You can read into that what you want."

"How old is their granddaughter? It'd be nice to have a friend the same age as my kids." I don't know why Mom didn't say *friend for Rose*, because that's what she meant. Rose was a friend magnet. Freddy and I didn't have

9

friends, didn't want friends, didn't need friends. We had each other.

"Not sure. I don't know them. I just know *of* them." Gloria tucked the tray under her arm. "Anyhoo. Is it just you and the girls and the duct-tape boy?"

"Just us and our dog, Jack. He's in the car," Rose said.

"You can't leave a dog in the car with this heat. He'll keel over!"

"He's already dead," I said. "We've got his ashes."

"Well, that's different. Folks here bury pets in the back-yard." Gloria winked at Rose. "After they're dead, of course."

Rose said, "I wanted to leave his ashes in the pond at the dog park in Lexington because he loved it there. But we had to leave fast. Some guy—"

"It just didn't work out," Mom said. "That's all."

It didn't work out because three days before we were supposed to leave, our neighbor told us a guy had been looking for Mom. That guy was going to take back our car because she ran out of money and stopped making pay-ments. We packed all night and sped out of town before sunrise. Mom said she was going to catch up on those bills once we got settled in Walnut Grove.

Then a man with a thick mustache yelled, "Gloria! If you want me to pay before I die, you better bring my tab."

"For chrissake, Harold, you get the same meal every time, and every time it's $5.99, and every time you write a check. So write a check and leave it on the table and add at least a dollar for a tip."

"A dollar! I grow soybeans, not money trees."

Gloria wandered to the man's table where they argued about whether he was cheap or she was greedy. Mom smiled at me, a smile as blinding as the sun. I wished her happiness was like a cold, and if she coughed hard enough, I'd catch it. So I looked out the window and tried to think like Mom and Rose, to see beauty. I saw an ocean of prairie grasses. The wind churned waves through the landscape, rolling the grasses toward a sky of endless blue. And it was beautiful in its own way.

But the view came with a new school. There would be new classmates and new teachers and new neighbors. For Mom and Rose, those things were shiny. For Freddy and me, they were just new—new and weird, new and scary.

When you constantly move, you know the world is big. But when you stare at the prairie sky, stretched across the Earth, unmarked by mountains or trees or buildings, you realize the world is bigger than you ever imagined.

So big it could swallow a girl.

· CHAPTER ·
TWO

The welcome sign said, WALNUT GROVE, MINNESOTA. CHILDHOOD HOME OF PIONEER AUTHOR LAURA INGALLS WILDER. Then it reminded visitors to PLEASE COME AGAIN, which sounded desperate, like the mayor worried people might never return.

Railroad tracks and power lines ran parallel to the highway, which pointed straight west, toward South Dakota and beyond. There was another diner near the welcome sign, and across from it were a silo and run-down buildings that looked like they'd once been used for farming. The voice on Mom's phone told us where to go—off the highway, a right turn through the main street, a left turn past a park, and a right turn into a neighborhood. The town was so small it reminded me of a little porcelain

Christmas village. Then the voice announced we'd arrived. Mom stopped in front of a neat, white one-story house with black shutters, which was literally the last house in town. The street went like this: house, house, house, house, cornfield.

Mom flashed a smile. "I have this sense of rich history just sitting here. Creativity thrives in places like this."

"It's like there's creativity in the air. I feel Laura's spirit," Rose said.

"Me, too," Mom said. "I've been called to the right place with the right project."

Rose gave Mom a high five. "You're going to write the best book ever, Mom."

"What about you two? Can you feel it?" Mom looked at Freddy and me in the back seat. Freddy pointed at his hearing aids and shrugged. I said, "Mom, if you make a million dollars on that book, I'll run up and down the street shouting that this is the right town at the right time."

"Deal," Mom said.

A woman with long black-and-gray hair waved to us from the door. Mom and Rose greeted her while Freddy and I stood by the car. When Mom realized we weren't there, she motioned us to join them.

"You must be Charlotte and Freddy." The woman spoke with a slight accent. "I'm Mia Ramos. Oh, what the heck!" She pulled Mom into an embrace. "I'm a hugger."

"So am I!" Mom laughed.

Rose squeezed between them. "I'm a hugger, too."

You saw that coming, right?

Freddy and I shared a perfectly reasonable aversion to hugging strangers. We stretched our cheeks into fake smiles. "You folks have a separate entrance for the basement through the garage. I'll give you a tour, then you can start getting settled," Mia said. "And you must have supper with us tonight."

"How nice!" Mom said as we packed into the narrow hall. "Thanks for letting us come a few days early."

Mia looked out the window. "You fit everything into your car?"

"Your ad said the basement is furnished. Whatever you have is all we need. It's too much hassle to move big stuff."

"Really? Well, that's different."

The wall in front of us was floor-to-ceiling covered with photos. Mia smiled when she saw me looking at the display. "Two sons, two daughters, six grandsons, three granddaughters, ten nephews, twenty nieces, three great-nephews, and three great-nieces."

"And a partridge in a pear tree," Mom said, and they laughed like old friends. Rose laughed, too.

Mia said, "You kids probably need to stretch your legs. Why don't you walk around town? Supper will be ready when you get back."

Rose decided to take the tour with Mom, so Freddy and I followed Mia's directions to the park. There was no traffic—just the sound of semitrucks rocketing down the highway a few blocks north. Across the street a woman stopped pulling weeds from her flowerbed to watch us. An old man peeked out his garage. Heads turned our way from every house, like a neighborhood of dominoes, all the way to the park.

Freddy and I watched kids play in the sandbox. The vow had been easy for Freddy—he didn't talk much in general. Mom didn't know until kindergarten that ear infections had messed up his hearing. All that time, I'd been his translator.

"You go first," I said.

"Okay." He thought for a few seconds. "The town is full of farmers and construction workers."

"Evidence?"

"Pickup trucks. As many pickup trucks as trees," Freddy said. "Now you."

I said, "Speaking of trees, the town was settled about one hundred fifty years ago."

"Evidence?"

"This is supposed to be the treeless prairie, right? But the town has big trees, trees that would need at least a hundred years to grow this tall. People had to bring them in and plant them. Now you."

"This is not going to be a budget-friendly city," Freddy said.

"It's a small town. Mom says she can make our money last twice as long here."

He cleared his throat. "You're doing it wrong."

"Okay, fine. What's your evidence?"

"Have you seen many churches? I haven't. We're going to be spending more money here than in Lexington."

Lexington was our favorite city because we lived in a neighborhood we called Church Row. At Trinity, Wednesday was youth group night. If we listened to bible stuff, we could eat cookies and play in the church's awesome game room. On Friday, St. John's had free family movie night in the community room with popcorn and candy. When Mom played at St. Catherine's guitar mass, we ate free meals at the spaghetti supper. Rose made friends with the granddaughters of the church ladies at Holy Redeemer, so we got leftovers from funeral lunches. Someone died in that church at least once a week. Also Lexington had a dog park and a theater that showed old movies for one dollar.

"That stinks," I said. "What if Mom needs to get a job? Where would she even work around here?"

"Maybe that diner."

Mom had always been a writer, but she'd never gotten paid for it until last month. She'd been a bus driver who wrote and a receptionist who wrote. A museum guide, a bartender, a propane delivery driver—all those things, but always a writer. She wrote before and after shifts. She wrote on the weekends. Finally a publisher bought her biography of Theodor Seuss Geisel, aka Dr. Seuss. She said the payment was small, but if we lived on a tight budget, she could quit working for a year and write a novel.

Tight budget? We only shopped at thrift stores; we never had cable; and Freddy, Rose, and I shared a cell phone. When we were little, Mom would take her guitar to the beach in Tampa. She'd play and we'd sing, and tourists would drop money in her guitar case. Then we'd use the money for gas.

Does a budget get any tighter?

Mom said Lexington and Church Row had everything we needed, and that we'd live there for many years. But she'd said that about Richmond, Charleston, Raleigh, and Atlanta. Mom has the attention span of a gnat, so when Laura's spirit beckoned her to Walnut Grove, we followed.

"You're Freddy and Charlotte, right?" A girl with light brown hair and charcoal eyes stood next to the bench.

Freddy elbowed me, and I said, "Um, yeah. Why?"

"I'm Julia. My grandma says you should come back for supper."

"Okay."

"Do you like spicy food? Grandma says she doesn't like too much spice, which is hilarious, because her enchiladas set off fireworks in your mouth."

"It's fine," I said.

"Did you walk through town? Did you see the museum? Did you see the school?"

I didn't know which question to answer, but it didn't matter, because she didn't stop talking the whole time we walked to the house. "The Laura Ingalls Wilder Museum is part of several buildings. There's a reconstructed church and school from the 1800s and a replica of Laura's house. Plus you can see inside a sod house, which is incredibly gross, don't you think? Living off the land is one thing; living *inside* the land is just creepy."

She took a breath, then continued. "Take my advice and stay out of the park. This new kid lives across the street. He crouches behind the slide and smokes, waiting for someone to pick on. His name is Chad, and he's like fifteen or something. We call him Bad Chad."

Julia talked too much. She tossed her long hair over her right shoulder, and a few seconds later, tossed it back to the left. I knew all about hair-tossers. Two hair-tossing girls in Richmond used to trip me on the playground. Also Julia's voice was high-pitched like a flute. She was a squeaky, hair-tossing motormouth. Freddy stared at Julia like his eyelids were tacked open. He usually looked away when people talked to him, but in Julia's case, he couldn't take his eyes off her. He was that annoyed. Twin Superpowers, right?

Finally we got to the house. I interrupted Julia's chatter about her grandmother's enchiladas and said, "We'll meet you inside. We need to get something out of the car."

When Julia opened the front door, I got the duct tape from the glove compartment and tossed it to Freddy. He tossed it right back.

"This stuff is sticky, Charlotte. It hurts to pull off. I'll just be quiet."

"Just make the ends of the tape stick to your cheeks. Don't press it against your lips."

"But we're eating. I'll have to take it off right away."

"What are you guys doing?" Julia shouted from the door.

I whispered to Freddy, "She needs to chill out."

He rolled his eyes and walked to the house.

Even though I understood Freddy's point about the tape, I suddenly felt cold. I actually shivered in the August sun. It was the timing of the eye roll. He should've rolled his eyes after Julia pestered us. But he didn't. He rolled his eyes *after* I said Julia needed to chill out.

I didn't think too much about it. I followed him into the house, knowing we were both annoyed—totally, completely, blindingly annoyed—by Julia Ramos.

We ate the enchiladas, rice and beans, and chocolate ice cream. Mom, Julia's grandfather Miguel, Rose, Julia, and Mia talked and laughed. I politely answered Mia's questions about what I liked at school (math), my favorite food (chicken strips), and the best place we'd lived (Lexington). And Freddy kept the vow. Our Twin Superpowers seemed intact.

But something was different.

Something was wrong.

I'd felt it while we walked from the park. I'd felt it when we stood by the car. And I felt it during dinner as Julia laughed and tossed her hair. But I shrugged off those feelings. It was just another new group of people in another new house in another new town.

What could possibly go wrong?

· **CHAPTER** ·

THREE

Mia and Miguel Ramos had tried to make the basement feel bright, a not-quite-a-basement basement, with white paint, floral furniture, and pictures of outdoor scenes hanging on the walls.

"Such beautiful art!" Mom smiled as she studied the picture of a creek cutting through prairie grasses. "Who needs windows when you can look at something this pretty?"

The stairs from the garage channeled down into the small kitchen, which was open to the living room. There were three tiny bedrooms and a bathroom. Despite the bright paint and flowers, it smelled and felt like a basement—musty and damp. But I didn't mind because we'd lived in worse places. Leaky ceilings, cracked windows, stained carpet. We'd had roach roommates in Tampa.

Or was it Raleigh?

Anyway, I helped Freddy set up his bedroom. We'd stopped sharing a room last year. Mom said we were getting older and needed privacy, which translated into me sharing a room with Rose and Freddy getting his own room. I tacked *Star Wars* posters on Freddy's wall while he shoved clothes into the small dresser.

"Observations?" I asked.

"Mia Ramos is going to make us fat."

"Evidence?"

"Her enchiladas rocked, and I heard Julia say she makes the best chocolate chip cookies ever," he said. "Go."

"Julia Ramos is annoying."

He shrugged.

"Evidence: she tosses her hair like someone in a shampoo commercial, and her voice sounds like a three-year-old playing a harmonica, and that waitress said her parents are a train wreck," I said. "Go."

He flopped onto the bed. "Our parents are a train wreck."

"Mom's not a train wreck. She's unique. And our dad might be a train wreck, or maybe he's not. We don't know."

"I guess."

All Mom told us about our dad is they met in Boston, and he broke her heart. We don't remember anything about him. She'd say, "He's not the man I thought he was." When we were babies, she'd moved us to Jacksonville, where she met Rose's dad, Reydel "Rey" Mendoza. He also was not the man she thought he was. Nor were any of her other boyfriends. At least Rey stayed in touch. He worked as a tour director on a cruise ship, which meant Rose went on Caribbean cruises at Thanksgiving, Christmas, spring break, and for a whole month in the summer. Freddy and I got a large collection of souvenir seashells out of the deal.

Rose came in carrying the black velvet bag that held the box of Jack's ashes. "Where should we keep Jack?" In our apartment in Lexington, Jack had been stored in a cupboard next to the flour and sugar. "Mom said in the bathroom cabinet with the toilet paper, but that's just not dignified."

"What about a drawer in our bedroom?"

"Mom thinks it'll make me sad to see Jack every time I get a pair of socks."

"She has a point," I said. "How about the top shelf of the closet in our room? Then he'll be close but not too close."

Rose beamed and left with the Jack bag. I sat next to Freddy. "We should convince Mom to get Rose another dog."

"We should," Freddy said. "You do the asking. I'll nod."

Our phone buzzed with a text message: *Hi! It's Julia. Want to get school supplies with us tomorrow?*

I glared at Freddy. "How'd she get our number?"

"She asked after dinner."

"You broke the vow?"

"I wrote our number on a piece of paper."

"Did you tell her about the vow?"

He shook his head. "I went with the laryngitis plan. I wrote that my throat hurt too much to talk."

Julia was confident. Too confident. Here's how I knew: She didn't say *my grandma said I should invite you*. She asked straight up. Those confident girls were mean. They said whatever they thought the second they thought it—and all their thoughts were obnoxious! Freddy and I were in for a long year of her badgering us if we didn't cut her off fast.

Know what I mean?

I started to reply, but Freddy grabbed my arm. "What are you going to say?"

"I'm going to tell her Mom is shopping while we unpack. You have a better idea?"

"No. Sounds good to me."

But Julia didn't give up. Two days later, while Freddy and I were binge-watching *The Hunger Games*, Julia sent another text. Freddy paused the movie. "Julia wants to know if we'll go to a water park tomorrow. Her grandma will drive us."

"Observation: Julia Ramos is a stalker."

Freddy sighed.

"Aren't you going to ask for evidence?"

"I already know your evidence, Charlotte. She texted us twice."

I hit him with the pillow from the couch. "So you want to go?"

Before he could answer, Mom and Rose came down the

stairs with shopping bags. Mom said, "Guess what? Mia wants to take everyone to a water park tomorrow. What a great way to spend your last day of summer vacation."

"The best way!" Rose said. "We were going to have a picnic on the real banks of the real Plum Creek by the Ingalls family's dugout. But we can do that next weekend instead."

"We don't want to go to a water park," I said. "We'd rather have a picnic."

That was how much Freddy and I dreaded going to a water park with Julia. We'd fake excitement about having a picnic on Laura's creek.

But Freddy pulled the little notebook and pencil from his back pocket. He scribbled a note and handed it to me. *There are leeches in creeks!*

I wrote, *There are Julias in water parks!*

He wrote, *Snakes! Ticks! Wolves! Bats! Who knows what else?*

I sighed and said to Mom, "Never mind. I guess we'd rather go to the water park."

Freddy handed me a second note. *Option B.* I nodded. We had a four-option plan for the vow of silence when we interacted with anyone from our new school. Duct tape was for home, for Mom. But duct tape at school meant bullying. So our plan was:

Option A: I talk for him.

Option B: Whenever possible, he'd pretend to have laryngitis.

Option C: If I wasn't there, or we'd overused the laryngitis plan, he'd shrug or nod or shake his head.

Disaster Option: If I couldn't help and he was forced to speak, he'd answer with the fewest possible words.

Mia drove us in her minivan to Fairmont, which was near the Iowa border. Walnut Grove was so small people had to go to Iowa to find a waterslide. Mom decided to go with us so she could visit with Mia.

Guess who was quiet during the entire drive?

Motormouth Julia! She leaned her head back while waiting for Tylenol to knock out a headache.

You'd think I'd turn joyful cartwheels.

You'd think I'd be able to relax instead of worrying about what to say to her.

Wrong.

This meant Mom had a very long and very quiet hour to talk to Mia.

"I'm calling my novel *Prairie Girl*. The main character is a young girl in the 1800s who's sent to live with relatives on the Minnesota prairie after her parents die. She's used to city life, so the adjustment is enormous."

"That sounds like a sad story," Mia said.

"Joy can't exist without sadness. That's why I connect with Laura Ingalls Wilder. She conveyed both the good and the bad, but she didn't let hard times get her down."

"I never thought about it like that."

I wanted to drown out the words with a drum solo.

Mom was gearing up to the part about how Laura's spirit had called her to Walnut Grove and I did not want Julia hearing that. "Will you turn up the radio? I like this song."

"I can barely hear your mother," Mia said. "Let me turn it off for a bit. Then you can pick a station. Okay?"

I looked back at Julia. She seemed to be napping, which was good. I did not want Julia hearing what Mom was saying because she might repeat it at school. You can't be invisible if your classmates learn about your mom talking to a dead pioneer girl.

Mom said, "I've been thinking about this story for years, but it felt locked inside me. Then I had a dream about Laura that helped me find the answer." Freddy's eyes opened wide and he elbowed me. But what was I supposed to do? Duct-tape Mom?

"What was the dream?" Mia asked.

"Laura and I had a picnic together and rode horses like we were best friends."

"Mom could literally smell the wildflowers," Rose said. "Right, Mom?"

"That's right, honey. All my senses were awakened." Freddy elbowed me again. I looked over my shoulder. Julia sat next to Rose in the back row. Her eyes stayed closed, so I shrugged at Freddy. Mom said, "Laura and I rode all the way to Walnut Grove. She faded into the horizon, but I stayed on the prairie and watched her leave. It was the most serene moment I've ever experienced. I knew immediately I needed to write my children's novel in Walnut Grove."

"Well, that's different," Mia said.

"So you moved here because of a dream?" Suddenly Julia was alert.

Mom laughed. "I wouldn't change my whole life because of a dream. That'd be ridiculous. I spent a lot of time connecting with Laura's energy. Then I made the decision."

"How do you connect with a dead person's energy?" Julia asked.

"It's like we're talking to each other," Mom said.

Freddy coughed and kicked my ankle.

I said, "In her book, the girl doesn't like the prairie. She wants to go back to the city, but eventually she learns to love the land. The end! Can we listen to the radio now?"

Mom turned around and looked at Julia. "The harvest is a metaphor for her growth. Do you think it's too quiet?"

"Is *quiet* another word for *boring*?" Julia asked.

Mom sighed. "I think you just answered my question. I've been researching, and everyone says quiet stories don't sell. You need dragons or wizards or vampires."

Julia said, "I like adventure stories."

"Maybe it can be quiet *and* exciting," Rose said. "You might think the *Little House* books are quiet because they're about prairies and pioneers, but they're not. There are fires and blizzards and diseases."

Mom said, "When the story growth is internal, inside

28

the character, that's when a story is truly exciting, don't you think, Julia? That's what I think."

Freddy face-palmed himself.

So I said, "I'd like to learn what kind of music gets played by radio stations on the prairie."

"Radio is radio. You moved to a new state, not a different planet." Mia chuckled and turned on the radio.

"A different planet?" Mom said. "What an interesting way to put it. That's something to think about. Definitely."

The way her voice trailed off made my stomach squeeze tight. I leaned forward so I could see her reflection in the rearview mirror. She had a faraway look in her eyes. It was the look Mom got before she quit a job, before she started packing, before she started a new project.

That look was never good.

. . . . .

The water park was small but it had everything you'd expect: a lazy river, fountains, a toddler section with a small slide that looked like a whale, and three spiral-shaped slides that dropped kids into the water. Julia and Rose went down the tallest slide over and over while Freddy and I floated on the lazy river.

Freddy's hearing aids were in the van, but he could hear me if I stayed close and spoke slowly.

"I think we have a problem, Freddy, and that problem's name is Mom-talks-too-much-about-spirits."

"We should've gone on that picnic. Julia's going to think I'm weird."

"I don't care if she thinks we're weird as long as she doesn't *tell* people we're weird. How do we handle Julia? School starts Monday. She won't forget all this stuff."

He thought about it. "If we were living in a spy movie, we could give her some memory-altering drugs."

"Or hypnotize her."

"What?"

"Hypnotize." I spoke louder. "We could hypnotize her."

There was a splash and suddenly Julia was next to us, clinging to my inner tube. Now I'd have to think of things to say, and that never worked out for me. When adults were stuck with strangers, they talked about gas prices or weather. But kids don't stand around saying things like, *How much did it cost you to fill your tank?*

"Don't you want to go down the slide?" Julia asked.

"Maybe later," I said. "The line is too long."

"Are you afraid of water?"

I shook my head. "I'd be at a picnic table if I was afraid of water."

Freddy mumbled something about going to the bathroom and swam to the edge of the pool. With Julia hanging on my tube, I couldn't kick fast enough to catch up to him.

"You can get your own tube," I said. "They're by the concessions."

When she flipped her wet hair, a thick strand smacked

my nose. "I'll just hang out while Rose is in the bathroom," she said. "So your mom wrote a book about Dr. Seuss? I love his books."

"Freddy and I think there's too much rhyming."

Julia said, "So you do not like his books. You do not like his looks. You do not like him here, you do not like him there, you do not like him anywhere. Get it?"

"I get it."

Her earrings sparkled in the sun. What kind of person wears earrings to a water park? Plus she had painted her fingernails and her toenails. They matched the pink in her swimming suit. Fashion girls were the meanest of all girls. "Where'd Freddy go?" she asked.

I shrugged and looked around. I saw him standing near the edge of the pool, like he was waiting for Julia to swim away. That made perfect sense—I was waiting for Julia to swim away, too—but something about the way he looked at her and shifted on his feet told me my Twin Superpowers might be confused.

Was he blushing? Or was his face pink from the sun?

Obviously it was the sun, right?

Obviously.

· **CHAPTER** ·

FOUR

When you're the new kid, the first day of school is the worst. It's bad for all students everywhere, because you're giving up summer, but being new adds an extra layer of stink. Every single time we start a new school, the other kids always talk about their summers while Freddy and I stare at our school supplies like we're fascinated by pencils.

Pencils!

That's how the first day in Mrs. Newman's class began: pencil staring. I waited until Mrs. Newman started talking before I studied the room. I never looked around while the kids were doing the summer-catch-up thing because I might make eye contact. I made that mistake in first grade, and this girl named Casey—or was it Lacy?—raised her hand and shouted to the teacher, "That weird girl is staring at me!" For months, kids told me to stop staring, even when my eyes were on the ground.

Even worse was second grade. I made eye contact with Molly Smith, which resulted in talking, laughing, play dates, and sleepovers. When we moved, she gave me a necklace with half a heart. It said *Best*. She kept the other half of the heart that said *Friends*. We cried and promised to write letters to each other. Then Mom lost her phone and everything on it, including Molly's address. All that time Mom told me not to worry because Molly had *my* new address. When Molly sent me a letter, it would have her address written in the corner of the envelope.

But a letter never came.

So, if you don't want to get bullied, avoid eye contact. If you don't want to get dumped, avoid eye contact. Look around during the teacher's welcome speech, which is what I did when Mrs. Newman started talking. Mrs. Newman had a big smile and small, squinty eyes. You can't trust a teacher smile. They're paid to flash teeth. That's why I always studied teachers' eyes, and Mrs. Newman had eyes like bullets. Mean eyes. The meanest I'd ever seen.

There were twenty-four students in our new class, including Julia, Freddy, and me. Six were Asian. Julia was the only Hispanic student, as far as I could tell. Everyone else was white. Eleven girls, thirteen boys. I'd need only a day or two to rank everyone on a popularity scale and sort them into the usual groups: cool kids, smart kids, extra-brainy kids with zero social skills, pre-jocks, and pre-cheerleaders. Freddy and I never fit in any group. We just floated above it all until we left.

Rose was different. Every time we started a new school, Rose was counting party invitations by the end of the first week. She could walk into a classroom and sniff out the popular kids. Then she charmed her way into the group.

You know that moment when you're not paying attention to an adult? When they sound like blah blah blah blah and then suddenly you hear a word bomb that gets your attention?

Well, Mrs. Newman dropped a word bomb: *Ingalls*.

"The folks at the Ingalls museum have an exciting new program. They're looking for a student to help with some projects throughout the school year. You'll have an opportunity to learn about the museum's artifacts and how to care for them. Please give your full attention to Mrs. Johnson."

I had been so busy looking at all the other students that I hadn't noticed a woman standing in the back of the room, a woman who seemed familiar. When she walked past my desk, I noticed the faint smell of fried chicken strips. It was Gloria from the Prairie Diner where kids eat free on Wednesdays.

Gloria—Mrs. Johnson—cleared her throat. "Kids, we're going to pick the winner based on an essay contest."

"The essay is going to be your first assignment. It's due next Monday," Mrs. Newman said. Nobody groaned, because nobody groans on the first day. "Mrs. Johnson will tell us what they're looking for."

"You will write about how Laura Ingalls and her story have influenced our community and affected your life." Gloria paused like she was letting tension build for an exciting conclusion. "You don't have to be a fan. I know there are students who haven't read the books, which saddens me greatly, but if you live here, there's no getting around Laura's influence. Even if you haven't read the books, which truly saddens me, you are aware of how she's shaped our town, and if you're not aware, that is heartbreaking."

Thinking about an essay contest made my head hurt. I rubbed my temples and closed my eyes. I had no interest in an essay contest about Laura Ingalls and some tiny town that couldn't accept the fact she died like one hundred years ago.

"Projects at the museum won't start until after Thanksgiving break. We've got a lot of cleaning to do, but we also need to update our records and send newsletters to the families who've donated artifacts throughout the years plus lots of other jobs. We've got inventory in the gift shop that—"

I yawned. Man, I was tired. So tired I could've dropped to the floor and napped right there.

Then I heard the words *five hundred dollars*. Suddenly I was alert. Everyone started clapping. Mrs. Newman said, "If your essay is selected, you can turn down the position and money, but the essay is required. It's an official assignment."

I thought about the things we could do with five hundred dollars. We wouldn't need churches. Mom could buy enough gas to drive to bigger towns for pizza and movies. We could get cable, or maybe buy a tablet. I was in. I could whip up a winning Laura Ingalls museum essay in an hour. Tops.

I already knew my competition would be Julia. She obviously was one of those overachieving students. I looked at Freddy, who sat in the corner of the back row, and waited for him to read my mind with his Twin Superpowers. I lifted my hand to get his attention, but he didn't notice. He was looking intently not at me, not at Mrs. Newman, and not at Gloria Johnson, but to the right. I followed his gaze to see where it landed.

Julia Ramos.

She was so annoying Freddy couldn't look away.

. . . . .

When you're a new kid, the first day of school is the worst, and the worst part of the worst day is lunch. First, you have to stand in line and not make eye contact, which isn't easy because everyone is literally inches apart. Second, you get a tray of unidentifiable meat and mushy vegetables, and they're not even decent vegetables like corn, but lima beans. Third, you have to find a place to sit.

That's the tricky part. You don't want to sit by the popular kids, because they're mean. Not in-your-face mean, but nasty in the way of saying things like, "Nice shirt! I had one just like it *three years ago*." Obviously you don't want to sit by a bully. You don't want to sit by the freaky kids or the brainy kids or the dumb kids. You want to sit by the kids who are on the verge of cool, but not too brainy, and definitely not freaky or dumb. Normally I'd need a week to sort it all out, but this school was the smallest I'd ever attended. I could easily do the rankings by the end of the day.

For now, though, I'd stick with Freddy. The good thing about this new school was that Walnut Grove was so small that Freddy and I were in the same class. We'd always gone to big schools, which meant we got separated. Teachers had this weird belief that twins should have time apart to "build their own identities," which is the how the principal in our old school described it.

Build our own identities?

Obviously they didn't know about Twin Superpowers. We were pretty much the same person.

In Walnut Grove, Freddy and I got to find an empty table together. Two tables away, Julia talked to Red Hair Girl and Purple Glasses Girl.

"Observation: Julia is one of those fake-nice kids." Freddy was too annoyed to ask for evidence, so I continued. "Evidence: she was really nice to us at dinner and at the water park, but now she's ignoring us."

Then Julia turned around and yelled, "Hey Freddy! Charlotte! I saved places for you."

"What do you want to do?" I whispered.

"We have to go, don't we?" Slowly he stood with his tray and looked around.

I followed him to Julia's table. She pointed at Red Hair Girl and Purple Glasses Girl. "These are my friends Emma and Bao. I was just telling them about you."

I couldn't stop myself from hoping she'd said nice things about us, like *those twins are funny*, but she probably told them about our mom talking to a dead pioneer girl.

We sat down, and the table filled up quickly with two other boys and two other girls: Crooked Glasses Boy, Floppy Bangs Boy, Girl with Braces #1, and Girl with Braces #2. Obviously they had names, but by the time we were at the next school, I'd forget the names but remember how they looked.

A good shortcut, right?

They all talked at once. Summer vacation, the high school football games, Minecraft, and the crimes Bad Chad the park bully had supposedly committed that summer— fighting, clogging the park bathroom, and throwing rocks at cars. Everyone seemed to know everyone and every- thing. All the talking made my headache worse.

Julia said to Freddy, "We go to the high school football games on Friday nights. I swear the whole town goes. You should come, too."

Freddy nodded, then shrugged.

"You still have laryngitis?" Julia asked. "You should see a doctor."

"My mom says there's an early flu going around," said Purple Glasses Girl.

"He gets laryngitis all the time," I said. "Our mom probably won't let us go Friday because he's been sick."

"Then you should come," Girl with Braces #1 said. "Everyone will be there. Do you want to?"

Was she setting me up? Like she'd get me to say yes and then she and her friends would laugh? I wasn't sure, so I shrugged. Then everyone started talking about the game, a chorus of voices, so I focused on my pile of lima beans. If I ate them slowly, one at a time, I could fill the rest of the lunch period with chewing instead of talking.

· CHAPTER ·

FIVE

The next morning, I woke up coughing, and my voice was scratchy. After making up the laryngitis story with Freddy, turns out I was sick—really sick. My head ached and my muscles ached and a cough rattled my bones from my skull to my toes. Mom pressed her hand against my forehead. "I hate having you miss the second day of school, but you're burning up."

"I'm fine, Mom." I couldn't send Freddy to school alone, especially with the vow.

In a panic, Freddy pulled out his notebook, scribbled some words, and showed it to Mom. "Sorry," she said. "I've taken a vow to not read notes. You'll have to tell me."

He gave the notebook to me. "It says, 'She looks fine. Give her some Tylenol.'" I started to stand. "I'm not that sick, Mom. I can go with him." I exploded into another coughing fit.

"Absolutely not."

"But I can't miss school already. I have to go."

"Not a chance. You need some ginger tea and a long nap." She led me to the couch and tucked a blanket around my lap.

Freddy sat on the couch next to me and whispered, "Observation: this is going to be the worst day ever."

"You're right. I don't even need to ask for evidence. I'm sorry, Freddy. If you have to say a few words, it'll be okay. Bring a cold lunch and eat in the bathroom."

"Good idea."

"It'll be fine."

Freddy bit his lip. "Really?"

"Really."

Freddy slapped a slice of cheese on bread and stuck the sandwich and a granola bar in his backpack. Freddy and Rose trudged up the stairs.

I snuggled into the couch with pillows and a blanket. Mom sat at the other end of the couch with a book, and I put my feet on her lap. "I'll read to you for a while." She showed me the book: *Little House in the Big Woods*, the first book in the series about Laura Ingalls's life.

"Perfect," I said.

"You must be delirious from fever. You don't even sound sarcastic."

I laughed, which made me cough. "There's an essay

42

contest at school about Laura. The winner gets five hundred dollars. I want a tablet. Or maybe you'd let us get a dog. I could pay for all the shots and food and everything."

"The tablet is a definite yes, but I'll have to think about the dog."

Mom read about Laura growing up in the big woods of Wisconsin with her older sister, Mary, and Ma and Pa. They had plenty of food and family nearby. They had dance parties and made candy from snow and maple syrup. Ma stopped a bear from attacking their cow. Pa played the fiddle and told stories about panthers. It was a nice story, a slow story, the kind of story you want to hear when you're snuggled on a couch.

"Mom, how does she remember all this stuff from when she's four or whatever? I can't remember preschool at all."

"She's probably putting together stories from her parents and sister and other relatives. Besides, it's a novel."

"But it's her life story, right?"

"A novelization of her life story." Mom put her hand on my forehead. "I'll read more later. Your fever is down, but I think you should nap."

Mom read to me between naps until Freddy and Rose came home from school. My Twin Superpowers told me his day had been awful—so awful he couldn't even tell me about it. He went straight to his room to do homework. I wondered if he'd hidden in the bathroom or if he'd sat alone at lunch. Then there was recess. I worried the boys were picking on him. Usually when kids saw the tiny wires around his ear, the questions started, and those questions led to teasing, and sometimes the teasing led to bullying. Once a boy asked Freddy if he could hear the sound of being punched; then he punched Freddy in the stomach.

Boys bully with their fists. Girls bully with their words. Weird, huh?

I didn't have to worry at all about Rose. She bounced out of friendships as easily as she bounced into them. In a year, we'd be moving, and Rose would never talk to her sleepover buddy again, or any of her Walnut Grove friends. She'd find a new group faster than we could unpack. Freddy and I had our Twin Superpowers. Mom connected with "energy in the universe," and Rose connected with every single person she met. Then she disconnected. Just like that.

For the next three days, I coughed and ached and worried about Freddy. But I couldn't talk to him. Mom made me go to my room when Freddy and Rose came home so I wouldn't spread the flu. Rose was sleeping with Mom all week. One morning before school, Freddy and I got a few minutes alone while Mom was in the bathroom.

"How's it going at school?" I asked him.

"I don't know. Fine, I guess. Not as bad as you would think."

"What do you mean?"

He rolled his eyes. It was the second time he'd rolled his eyes at me. The first time was when Julia had hassled us about eating dinner. He'd started an eye-rolling kick—that's

how bad his week was going. I knew from my Twin Superpowers, though, that he just didn't want me to worry about
him. He was worried about *me* being so sick.

"Why aren't you using the tape at night?" I asked.

"Mom threw it away."

"Figures," I said. "But you're not talking, right?"

"Hardly at all."

I crossed my arms. "What does that mean?"

"Mom is scheming. She keeps sending me upstairs with
stuff so I have to talk to Julia."

"Like what?"

"First it was cookies. Then I had to borrow eggs. Yesterday it was next month's rent check."

"Mom paid rent *early*?" The shock set off a coughing jag.

Freddy gave me a glass of water and patted my back. "I
better not be late." He headed up the stairs before my
cough settled down.

I snuggled into the couch and waited for Mom to read
more Laura. So far, I'd heard about Laura's family moving
to the Kansas prairie. For Christmas, Laura and Mary got
their very own cup, a piece of candy, and a shiny new
penny. They thought it was the best Christmas ever. Then
everything went wrong. A neighbor almost died in their well,
Pa almost died in a blizzard, and the whole family almost
died from fever 'n' ague.

What even is that?

I'd asked Mom if I had fever 'n' ague. She'd laughed

and said fever 'n' ague was malaria, and practically no one in the United States ever gets it. I had the regular old flu.

And Ma, who is the sweetest character in the book, hates Indians, and I mean hates hates hates them. Maybe it was because the Ingallses built their cabin on Indian land, and the Indians weren't too happy about it. In the end, both the Indians and the Ingallses pack up their stuff and move. The Indians are forced to leave their hunting lands, and the Ingallses end up on the banks of Plum Creek near Walnut Grove, because all Pa wants to do is move. That man will not stay in one place.

Here's what you call irony: Laura and Mary meet a nasty girl in Walnut Grove named Nellie Oleson. She's like the pioneer version of Julia, all nice around adults but mean to the kids. Then everything goes wrong *again*. The Ingallses have to live in a hole in the ground called a dugout, the grasshoppers eat their crops, and Pa almost dies in another blizzard.

Have you ever wondered why adults always act like weather is a big deal? Read the *Little House* books.

When Mom stopped reading to make lunch, I took notes for the Laura essay. It wasn't going to be easy to explain how Laura influenced Walnut Grove, because we'd only just arrived. But I could write about how we were alike. The Ingalls family moved all the time. We moved all the time. Laura was a writer, and Mom was a writer. Laura had a sister named Mary who acted perfect. I had Rose. Laura had Nellie. I had Julia. She had fever 'n' ague. I had the flu. If Laura was alive, we'd have Twin Superpowers.

On Friday, Mom didn't want to read anymore. "I'm feeling a little tapped out, a little restless," she said. "I need fresh air. Will you be okay if I take a long walk?"

"Sure."

"Maybe I'll bring my laptop and work at the diner for a while."

"How's the book coming? You've hardly been on your laptop at all."

Mom took off her glasses and used the bottom of her T-shirt to clean them. "Writing takes place in the head, too. Thinking and daydreaming are part of the process."

I thought about her expression in the van the day Mia drove us to the water park. Maybe that's why Mom got that faraway look. She was thinking and daydreaming.

"Reading Laura to me is good inspiration, right?"

"Yes." She shrugged. "And no."

"It can't be yes *and* no. That makes no sense."

"You can't rush these things. I've been meditating. I've been using my crystals. But I'm changing the book, and the plot needs to simmer in my mind." It sounded like Mom wasn't getting Laura's mystical messages through the energy of the universe, and that meant something was wrong.

"What kind of changes?"

"I'm not sure yet."

Mom's face looked normal, and her body language

looked normal, but the air around us felt heavy, almost clogged.

I thought I'd have a whole weekend to talk to Freddy about it, but Mom messed that up, too. On Saturday morning Mom told us Mia was taking Julia to Minneapolis to shop for school clothes, and since Freddy was outgrowing everything, she was accepting Mia's invitation for him to go along.

Schemer! Mom was definitely trying to break Freddy's vow.

Freddy wrote something in his notebook and handed it to Mom. She said, "I've taken a vow to not read notes, remember? You'll have to tell me."

Freddy gave me the notebook. "He says, 'Did they really invite me or did you ask if I could go? Because that would be weird.'"

"Mia did the asking."

"What about me?" Rose asked. "I need clothes, too."

"You have a wardrobe that fits, and so does Charlotte. Have you noticed that every single day Freddy wears a rock-and-roll T-shirt with a hoodie?"

"That's what he likes," I said.

"Maybe he wants to change it up," Mom said. "They're going to the Mall of America."

Rose frowned. "They're not even going to thrift stores?"

"So much for Mom's opposition to corporate greed," I grumbled.

"We all deserve an occasional treat," Mom said. "A very rare treat. You girls will get a turn. I promise."

"Mom, we all know this is part of your plan to trick Freddy into talking," I said. "I guess you're willing to spend a lot of money to break the vow. But he won't."

"He's getting sixty dollars, and he knows to look for the clearance racks."

Freddy scribbled another note, which I read. "He says, 'I don't want to shop with a girl. She'll think I'm weird.'" I could picture Freddy standing in the girls' section, his face burning red from embarrassment, while Julia and her mother looked at cute shirts, or worse, bras! And I wouldn't be there to save him.

"Maybe I should go with them," I said. "I don't have to buy anything. I'll get stuff for myself when I win the essay contest."

"You need to rest."

"I'm pretty much over fever 'n' ague."

Mom ignored me. "Embrace the adventure, Freddy, and figure out who you are. This is a magical time in life. Enjoy it." She smiled and squeezed his shoulder. "Also, there's another surprise. You're going to spend the night at Mia's sister's house and return Sunday evening. Julia has cousins your age, so you'll be meeting more kids. More conversations, more friends, more fun."

"Nice plan, Mom. You are the master," I said. "But he still has laryngitis, if you know what I mean."

Mom smiled. "We'll see about that."

Rose smiled. "It'll be good for you, Freddy. Charlotte can get new clothes later, because fair is fair, and I'll get money from Daddy for clothes so Mom has more to spend on you guys. Everything works out, right?"

Mom and Rose hugged.

Rose crossed her arms and stomped her foot. "But I don't feel like leaving early."

It was Monday morning, and all I wanted was a few minutes alone with Freddy to catch up. I needed him to tell me about the week at school, and the trip to the Mall of America with Julia, and whether the laryngitis plan preserved the vow of silence.

Suddenly Rose wanted to walk with us. I said, "You always rush to school to talk to your friends."

"Maybe today I'm feeling different."

"Feel different tomorrow. Today Freddy and I want to talk. Privately." I stretched out the word *privately*. "We'll be right behind you. As soon as Freddy gets out of the bathroom, we'll leave."

Rose pinched her lips together, clomped up the stairs, and slammed the door behind her. By the time Freddy and I left the house, her angry march had propelled her four blocks ahead of us.

"What's with her?" Freddy asked.

"She's mad, but I'll make it up to her. I'll win that essay contest and buy us a dog."

"Seems unfair we have to write about Walnut Grove when we just moved here. I can't even say Mom is a writer inspired by Laura because she changed her whole book. Did you know that? It's all different now."

"She mentioned something. How different?"

"The orphan on the prairie is gone. Now she's writing about twins who sneak aboard this space shuttle that's going to colonize Mars."

I almost tripped. "No way! She said the orphan story was the book of her heart."

"It's not the book of her heart anymore. She told me last week. You were napping." He shrugged. "You know what? I'd rather read an exciting space book than a boring prairie book. Besides, Mom says it's the same story because it's about exploration and pioneers. So we're still here for Laura. She still needs Laura's spirit."

"The prairie wasn't boring. The Ingalls family faced death every week."

Freddy smiled. "I have an observation: our mother knows nothing about science."

"Evidence?"

"She was shocked when I told her there used to be water on Mars, but it's now frozen in the soil. She thought I was some kind of science genius. I told her every first grader knows that."

I didn't laugh. "Why didn't you tell me about this right away?"

"Mom practically built a moat around your room."

We were about a block from school at that point. Julia waved at us from the steps of the building. Freddy said, "I'm going to run ahead. I've got to check my essay, and it's in my locker."

"But—"

And he was gone. I couldn't run to catch up. I was still tired and weak from the fever 'n' ague. By the time I got inside, Freddy was standing in front of his locker, looking at a sheet of paper. I was going to look at his paper, too, but Spiked Hair Boy and Boy Who Needs Braces got in front of me. "Hey, Red Fred!"

My chest burned. Barely a week into the school year and Spiked Hair Boy and Boy Who Needs Braces had already picked Freddy as their victim. I wanted to smack those boys for teasing him, but then Boy Who Needs Braces said, "I thought you were coming to the football game."

"We sacked the other team," Spiked Hair Boy said.

Freddy stuck to the vow. He didn't say a word. I thought about ordering them to leave him alone, but girls couldn't stick up for boys. It made the boy look weak, and bullies could smell weakness. This was a school commandment: sisters shalt not defend thine brothers. Finally Freddy shrugged and darted into the classroom.

Spiked Hair Boy said, "What's his deal?"

Boy Who Needs Braces shrugged. "I don't know. Maybe he was grounded or something."

"But he said he was going." They walked to class together.

He'd *said* he was going?

Something was definitely different.

Something was definitely wrong.

You know what it's like when you realize everything you know, you absolutely *know*, turns out to be a fat mistake?

Your ribs squeeze your heart until it stops beating. Your legs shake. Your insides twist and turn like clothes in a dryer. And your eyes fill with tears no matter how hard you try to hold them back.

That's what it's like.

Freddy had not only talked to those boys; he'd accepted an invitation to go to a football game. *Red Fred* wasn't an insult. It was a nickname—a dumb nickname considering he had blond hair. And he'd kept all of it secret from me.

During one short week, our Twin Superpowers had evaporated. I got fever 'n' ague. Freddy got friends.

Julia brushed against me and said, "Is Freddy here?"

I stared at my feet until she gave up and went to class. I didn't know what to do. Lunch was in three hours—just three short hours until I had to find a place to sit, and it looked like I couldn't sit with "Red Fred" because he already had plans. Then there was the walk home alone and the walk to school the next day and another lunch and everything multiplied by days and weeks and months until Mom finished the book and we packed our stuff into the car.

And suddenly I knew something with absolute clarity. As much as I wanted to blame Julia or those boys, it wasn't their fault we moved to Walnut Grove. We came because of Laura Ingalls and her dumb books.

I nearly slammed into Mrs. Newman as I entered the classroom. She gave me her teacher smile—the kind that says *I'm paid to be nice to you.* "Welcome back, Charlotte. Let's talk before lunch about how to get you caught up. The essays are due today, but I can give you a few extra days."

Hah. I wouldn't work at that stupid museum for one million dollars. In fact, if I had a million dollars, I'd *buy* the museum just so I could tear it down.

"That's okay. I don't need more time." I went to my desk and pulled out a notebook. I wrote furious words:

Laura Ingalls Essay
By Charlotte Lake

LAURA INGALLS IS RUINING MY LIFE!!!!!!

I ripped the sheet out of the notebook, marched to Mrs. Newman's desk, and put it in the wire basket marked *Laura Ingalls Essay Contest.*

I looked at Freddy only one time all morning, and he was staring at Julia. Julia! Obviously he couldn't see she was fake-nice. He was blinded by her hair-tossing.

At lunch I hid in a stall in the bathroom. If I saw Freddy, oops, make that *Red Fred*, I'd hit him or cry or both. Freddy knew where I was—our Twin Superpowers could lead him to me, if he wanted to be led, and he could bang on the door and yell my name, but he obviously didn't care.

When the horrible day ended, I ran home. Even though I felt tired and hungry and I started coughing halfway there, I pumped my legs until I was in the basement.

Mom was sitting in the recliner with her laptop. "Hi, sweetie. Where's Freddy?"

"Ask Julia Ramos."

"What's wrong?"

I wasn't going to tell her about Red Fred. She'd be happy Freddy was making "connections in the world." But I did have a question—an important question. "Mom, did you throw away Freddy's duct tape?"

She blinked a few times. "Of course not. I believe children should be free to express themselves. Why?"

See?

He was a liar, too!

"No reason."

In my bedroom I took the Jack bag from the closet. Jack was a mutt—Mom guessed a mix of terrier and poodle or cocker spaniel. We'd found him in the alley by our apartment in Richmond. He was so dirty that when we washed him we were shocked to discover he wasn't brown. He was white with brown patches. Rose had been begging for a dog, so Mom concluded Jack's appearance was a sign from the universe. We'd lived in apartments with no-pets policies, but our neighbors never ratted us out or complained, because who would do that to Rose, the adorable people magnet? Rose who gave neighbors hand-made birthday cards, holiday cards, and you're-a-great-neighbor cards; Rose who handed out cookies; Rose who cleaned up Jack's turds as fast as he produced them.

Nobody would do that to Rose. Even crabby Mr. Thompson, with fierce eyes and a gruff voice, didn't complain.

Or was his last name Thomas?

Anyway, we brought Jack home, and during the first two weeks, Mom had Rose carry dog treats in her pockets all the time. Jack followed her everywhere. Freddy and I could snuggle with Jack and play with him, but only Rose got to feed him and reward him with treats. When it came to connection building, Mom obviously trusted bacon chews more than the universe.

But we'd all cried when Jack died. Even though he was Rose's dog, he knew, he always knew, when one of us was having a bad day. He would climb on our laps and lick our faces, and not because we'd just eaten cheeseburgers, but because he could tell something was wrong.

Jack was a small dog, a lap dog.

How could his ashes be so heavy?

The knock on my bedroom door was Freddy. "Mom says it's almost time to eat." I didn't answer. He looked at his feet while he spoke. "Charlotte, it's complicated."

"Yeah. It's complicated all right."

"Maybe I can keep the vow at home but without the tape."

"Mom didn't throw the tape away, Freddy. You did."

He crossed his arms. "Hey, it was your idea anyway. Why don't you do it if you think it's so easy?"

"It was not my idea."

"Yes, it was. At first it was a joke, then you were all into it. You gave me the notebook because it fit in my pocket."

"I gave you the notebook after you decided to do it. After!"

Mom opened the door. "Sounds like an exception to the vow has been made."

"We're talking privately," I said.

"Fine. Dinner in five minutes."

Freddy waited for Mom to leave before speaking. "It started the first day you were sick. Ethan was talking to me on the way to lunch, so I couldn't just rush into the bathroom. Then at the table, all the guys were telling their favorite jokes, and they said it was my turn. I had to say something. So I was like, 'Knock knock,' and Christian said, 'Who's there?' And I said, 'Smell mop.' And he said, 'Smell mop who?' It was dead quiet for a few seconds, and I was wishing that the ground would swallow me. Then Ethan said, 'Smell my poo? That's hilarious!' Suddenly everyone got it and started laughing. They laughed so loud one of the lunch ladies told us to turn down the volume. They weren't laughing at me, Charlotte. They were laughing at my joke."

I crossed my arms. "You like Julia."

"I don't *not* like her."

"Which means you like her."

"It means I like her, but I don't like her, like her. She's just nice. Nothing else."

I was not letting him off the hook. "Tell me, Freddy, does she have pierced ears?"

"Yeah. So?"

"Did she wear fingernail polish that day we went to the water park?"

"Yeah. So?"

I stomped my foot. "When have you ever noticed pierced ears and fingernail polish? You like her."

"You could like her, too."

"I don't like fake-nice people."

Then Rose called us to dinner. I put Jack back in the closet while Freddy stomped to the table.

We gathered over a meal of overcooked spaghetti with bland tomato sauce. The mood was dark. Freddy shoveled food in his mouth. I picked at my piece of garlic bread. Only Rose talked. She happily chatted about how Laura Ingalls didn't start writing her books until she was an old lady living on her farm in Missouri. Mom just nodded and sighed occasionally.

Mom was not someone who simply nodded and sighed.

Mom was a talker. And when it came to Laura and writing, she could talk endlessly.

Why was she being so quiet?

I figured Mom knew Freddy and I were fighting, and she felt bad our Twin Superpowers had been disrupted.

After dinner, I learned what was really bothering her. Mom asked Rose to take cookies she had baked upstairs to Mia. Then she told me and Freddy to sit on the couch because we needed to have a quick talk about Rose's dad.

"Rey called and told me he's getting married. Rose doesn't know yet." Mom let out a long, frustrated sigh. "Honestly I'm happy for him, but it's going to be a shock to Rose."

"I didn't even know he had a girlfriend," I said.

"He met her on the ship. She's Greek. He's going to be on his honeymoon over Thanksgiving, so Rose won't get to see him. She'll be heartbroken. It's her special time with him."

"That stinks," I said. Freddy nodded.

"It gets worse. He's going to meet his new wife's family in Greece over Christmas, and they're quite conservative. Apparently they're not thrilled he's a divorced man with a child. He said it's not the right time to have Rose come with them."

"So she won't see him at Thanksgiving or Christmas?"

"She'll be heartbroken. I'm going to let the Thanksgiving news settle before I tell her about Christmas. I'm hoping he'll change his mind," Mom said. "Please be extra sensitive with Rose. She'll get strength from the love we give her."

We were all silent for a moment.

Mom looked downright gloomy. Mom never looked gloomy. In fact, she looked like she'd skipped washing her hair. I didn't like this gloomy, sighing, unwashed version of my mother. It made me worry. So I said, "There's one good thing. At least we get to have Rose with us for the holidays."

"That's my girl." Mom hugged me.

I'd just made a rainbow from the rain. Me! Charlotte Lake, observer of gray skies.

I hate to admit it, but it felt good to have a Rose moment, you know?

. . . . .

All night I worried about the cafeteria. I'd missed the week when kids came up with the unofficial seating chart. If I wasn't careful, I could end up near the bullies or the freaky kids. I couldn't eat in the bathroom every single day. And if I skipped lunch, my stomach might roar in math class and everyone would laugh at me.

On the embarrassment scale, stomach growls are worse than hiccups but better than burps, right?

I had no choice but to bring a sandwich and eat in a bathroom stall.

Turns out, I didn't have to worry about what I would do for lunch, because when everyone left for the cafeteria, Mrs. Newman beckoned me to her desk and handed me a blank piece of paper. "I want a revision of your essay. I applaud your writing. Succinct writing is underappreciated. Most people think length somehow relates to quality, and I'm impressed you recognize the fallacy."

"Fallacy?"

"It means mistaken belief. Charlotte, you don't have to write a single positive word about Laura Ingalls. But if you're telling me Laura Ingalls is ruining your life, I want a thorough explanation."

I was so consumed by my fight with Freddy, and then worried about how to face all the kids, that I didn't think about Mrs. Newman and the essay I'd put in the basket. Of course she was going to have something to say about my essay! What difference did it make? It was just a dumb contest.

"Charlotte?"

I nodded.

"I want a verbal acknowledgment that you understand."

"I understand."

"Good."

I wrote the essay during lunch in the classroom. It didn't take long, because it is a fallacy that the amount of time spent on an assignment relates to its quality.

Laura Ingalls Essay
By Charlotte Lake

I will thoroughly explain how Laura Ingalls is ruining my life. My mother is a writer. Actually, she's a lot of things. She's been a school bus driver, a lab technician, and a forklift operator. She even worked at a funeral home. But you won't find Mom's hero on a bus or in a lab, warehouse, or funeral home. To understand Mom's hero, you'd have to go to the Minnesota prairie, because her hero is Laura Ingalls Wilder.

You said concise writing is underappreciated. I will show you how it is not a fallacy to be both concise and thorough. Here are concise but thorough sentences about my mother, Martha Lake, and Laura Ingalls.

1. Laura Ingalls was a bestselling author. My mother wants to be a bestselling author.

2. Laura Ingalls wrote books for kids. My mother wants to write books for kids.

3. Laura Ingalls wrote about a child in the 1800s. My mother wants to write about a child in the 1800s.

4. Laura Ingalls wrote about the prairie. My mother wants to write about the prairie.

Therefore, we moved to the prairie to find inspiration. She believes Laura's spirit will guide her. She believes lots of crazy things like lavender oil cures anxiety and your personal energy affects the universe. My family has moved so many times I've lost count, but we've never lived in a town with 800 people and no malls or movie theaters or beaches or NOTHING to do. We are city people. Lexington, Kentucky, is the coldest place we've ever lived, and I've heard Minnesota is worse. It's possible to die in cold weather. And I mean that literally. And when I say literally, I mean the correct use of literally and not the common use in which people say literally but mean figuratively.

You could argue that my problems are not Laura's fault. You could argue that my mother is at fault. Here's a compromise: they can share the blame. My mother is ruining one half of my life. Laura Ingalls is ruining the other half.

I took the essay home with me in case I changed my mind. I didn't change my mind.
But you knew that, right?

· CHAPTER ·
SEVEN

I ignored Freddy all week, and he ignored me right back, like we'd taken vows of silence against each other.

Turns out I didn't have to eat lunch in the bathroom stall, either. Working on the essay during lunch gave me an idea—a great idea. Since I had the flu for a week, I pretended I was so far behind that I had to eat lunch in the classroom to catch up. Nothing really happens the first week of school, but I acted like I had no idea what we were doing in class. I acted like I'd missed months of school, like I could barely remember basic addition and subtraction.

On Friday, Mrs. Newman sat in the desk next to me while everyone headed to lunch. "We need to talk, Charlotte. If you're still behind, maybe we should see about getting you some extra help."

"I just work slow. Everything's fine."

"Kids need breaks during the day. We learn best when we have a chance to eat lunch, get outside, and talk to friends."

"I'm . . . sensitive to the cold, and it's been unseasonably cold. That's what the radio said. It's like I get sick whenever I'm in cold weather."

"Are you having problems with the other kids? Maybe I can help. It's very hard to be in a new school at your age." Mrs. Newman was using her I-care-about-you smile and her I-don't-care-about-you eyes.

"It's not. I'm used to new schools."

"It's also hard to live up to a very popular brother."

Yes, those were her exact words: *Very. Popular. Brother.*

"It's not hard. I just like to read when I eat."

She crossed her arms. "Beginning next week, you need to eat lunch in the cafeteria with the other kids and get outside and enjoy the weather. Trust me, winter comes quickly here."

When the last bell rang, I rushed out of school to avoid Julia and Freddy, who apparently decided to become walking buddies. When I got home, Mom was sitting on the couch with her arm around Rose, whose face was wet with tears.

"What's going on?" I asked.

"I was just telling Rose about her dad getting married and how happy I am for him and how having a stepmother will be a beautiful experience. Now she'll have two moms who love her."

Rose didn't look convinced. "He's going on a honeymoon at Thanksgiving, and I'm not invited."

"Because nobody goes on a honeymoon except for the husband and wife. You can't go. It's practically a law," I said.

"I guess." She wiped her face with the bottom of her shirt. "I hope she's not awful."

"Your dad wouldn't marry an awful person." Mom hugged her.

"Not a chance," I said.

Rose took a deep breath and nodded. "You're right. Dad married you, and you're the best person in the world, so maybe his new wife is the second best. Guess I'll find out at Christmas."

I looked at Mom. She shook her head and mouthed the word *no*. Obviously she believed Rey would change his mind and take Rose to Greece. I thought Mom should dump all the bad news at once, but I guess rainbow-finders think differently.

"Where's the sleepover tonight, Rose?" I asked. "A night with a friend will cheer you up."

"Leah had to cancel. She's sick."

Mom said, "Charlotte, I want you to go to the football game tonight with Julia and Freddy."

"No, thanks."

"Honey, you have to open yourself to opportunities. You have to live with joyful intention."

Joyful intention? What even is that?

"I don't like football. Besides, Rose is staying home. We'll have a girls' night." The phrase didn't roll off my tongue. I don't think I'd ever said *girls' night* before, because *girls' night* meant a night without Freddy. I couldn't remember the last time Freddy and I hadn't been together on a Friday night, either watching movies or playing games or eating pizza. "Just you, me, and Rose. How awesome will that be?"

Rose's face lit up. "Very awesome. See? You don't need Freddy. I'll be your sidekick."

I didn't know what to say to that. Thankfully Mom spoke first. "I'll agree to this girls' night on one condition: I plan our evening."

. . . . .

I should've asked for details, because as soon as Freddy left for the game, Mom dropped her plan on us. "I haven't been out of the house. I've been sleeping too much. It's not like me. I need a strong dose of Laura. An extra-strong dose. So we're going to the real banks of the real Plum Creek—"

"What?"

"—and we're going to make a fire—"

"Why?"

"—and we're going to roast marshmallows and eat s'mores."

"What? Why?" I looked at Rose for help, but she wore an ear-to-ear grin.

But you knew that, right?

I said, "I'm still recovering from fever 'n' ague."

Mom pulled off her ponytail binder and let her hair fall in waves down her back. "The basement is making me claustrophobic. I need to breathe and see the sky. I need space and air."

"Me, too," Rose said. "Space and air."

I had tried to escape the football game with this girls' night idea and look where it got me. Laura's creek! I sighed. "Fine. Space and air."

We had marshmallows and graham crackers but no chocolate, so we stopped at the gas station for candy bars. The cashier put down the magazine he'd been reading and studied us. "Are you the writer who moved to town?"

Mom looked around the store, apparently for the other writer who'd moved to town. I nudged her. "He's talking about you, Mom."

"Me?" She blushed. "Well, I'm a writer, and I just moved to town, so yes, I'm a writer who moved to town."

"How'd you know?" I asked.

"My neighbor said a lady writer and her kids moved to town from Kentucky. You've got a Kentucky license plate on your car. I'm a gas station manager by night and detective by day."

"Are you really a detective?" Rose asked.

He laughed and lifted his Minnesota Twins baseball cap to scratch his head. "No, but I am indeed a gas station manager. Name's Ted but everyone calls me Shorty."

"But you're tall," Rose said.

He nodded. "And that's why they call me Shorty."

"An ironic nickname. That's cute." Mom laughed a little and blushed.

Mom was always talking about irony in books, but she never used the word *cute*. She never blushed while using the word *cute*. I didn't see what was so cute about unusual nicknames. I figured it was a small-town thing. Freddy had blond hair and brown eyes like me, but kids called him Red Fred. Then there was Bad Chad. And Boy Who Needs Braces had an Asian name—something like Chue— and everyone called him Chuck.

Rose said, "My mom's name is Martha, and I'm Rose, and my sister is Charlotte, and we have a brother named Freddy, and we live with the Ramos family."

"Better you folks than their daughter and that rotten son-in-law. He brought a suitcase full of trouble to town." He shook his head. "I better shut my trap."

"What trouble?" Rose asked.

"Rose!" Mom hushed her. "How much do I owe you, Ted?"

"Call me Shorty."

"How much do I owe you, Shorty?"

"Tonight the treats are on me."

"That's so nice." Mom blushed again. "Thank you."

"You bet," he said. "Welcome to Walnut Grove, Martha-the-writer-from-Kentucky."

．．．．．

By the time we got to the creek, it was dark. We parked on the shoulder of the road and walked down a narrow strip of gravel. Mom said, "Mia told me the site is private property now, but the owners have left this section open for Laura fans to explore."

"She also said you're supposed to put some money in the little box in the parking area to help with expenses," Rose said.

"I parked on the highway, so we're fine. Did you bring the flashlights?"

I clicked the flashlight and waved the beam around. The ground sloped upward until it met a cluster of trees. The crickets and frogs were so loud I couldn't hear the creek.

Mom said, "There's a sign marking the dugout's location on the other side of the creek. Mia said there's a walking bridge."

"Can we actually look inside the dugout?" I asked.

Rose laughed. "Listen to her, Mom. She thinks it's still here."

I frowned. Rose was making fun of me. The world really had gone topsy-turvy. "Perhaps you can enlighten me with your deep knowledge of all things Laura."

"Mom, Charlotte's being sarcastic."

"Let's assume Charlotte has the best intentions and truly wants information. Then you can answer with kindness and generosity."

"Fine. The man who sold this land to the Ingallses made the dugout. He literally dug a hole in the hillside and built some kind of front for it and slapped on a door. There's no way something like that would last 150 years. It collapsed, but there's sort of an indentation left."

"Thanks for your kindness and generosity, Rose," I said.

"Girls, please." Mom's voice was firm. We followed her down a narrow path that appeared to have been mowed. On both sides of us, the prairie grasses were waist high. The path split into two directions. I walked straight ahead, into the weeds, to take a look. Mom pulled me back. "Be careful. You could walk off the bank and end up in the water. I think Mia said go to the left."

In a minute we were on a wooden walking bridge. I scoped out the creek with my flashlight. The water was still and dark. I said, "It's creepy. Maybe it's haunted."

"It's serene." Mom said. "It's living history. I really needed this. Just close your eyes and listen to the crickets and the frogs. These are the exact same sounds Laura heard 150 years ago." A horn blasted from the road, and she laughed. "Except for that."

On the other side of the bridge was a sign towering in the weeds. With the flashlight we could make out yellow letters. THE CHARLES INGALLS FAMILY'S DUGOUT HOME WAS LOCATED HERE IN THE 1870S. THIS DEPRESSION IS ALL THAT REMAINS SINCE THE ROOF CAVED IN YEARS AGO. THE PRAIRIE GRASSES AND FLOWERS HERE GROW MUCH AS THEY DID IN LAURA'S TIME AND THE SPRING STILL FLOWS NEARBY.

"Told you," Rose said.

I shined the light in her face. "You're a regular encyclopedia."

"Magical, isn't it?" Mom's voice sounded dreamy. "I feel better already."

"It feels like she's here, like if we close our eyes we could hear her splashing in the creek," Rose said. "Listen."

Mom squeezed my hand. "Are you listening, Charlotte? Enjoy this. Use these moments for your essay contest."

"I'm already done. Besides, if they paid me a million dollars, I wouldn't work in Laura's museum."

"I thought you were enjoying her books," Mom said.

"I just want you to write the Mars book so we can go back to . . ." I almost said *to the way things used to be*, but I caught myself. ". . . to Church Row."

"Better yet," Rose said, "go back to the prairie book. The Mars idea just isn't *you*."

Mom shined the flashlight in my face. "Charlotte, take a moment to refocus. Turn off the negativity and let yourself experience the moment."

I sighed. I suddenly didn't feel like arguing anymore. "Fine. This place is . . . interesting."

That made her happy. "Isn't it? Let's gather firewood. It's cold. We can snuggle around the fire and take all of this in."

We crossed the bridge, went down the path, and then fanned in different directions using the flashlights to search for wood. People in wilderness movies are always gathering firewood. In a few minutes they're sitting around a crackling fire. Maybe that's how it works in a forest, but this was the prairie. And maybe it works like that if you know what you're doing, but we did not. Trees towered along the creek, but they hadn't shed perfectly sized logs. With our flashlights guiding the way, we searched the tangle of weeds.

"How's this?" We turned our flashlights to Rose, who was holding a stick.

"Too small," Mom said.

"It could be kindling."

Mom said, "Keep looking. If we get enough sticks, it'll probably work."

I was tempted to make fun of Rose's sudden prairie vocabulary. *Kindling*? But I reminded myself about her dad and kept quiet. If Freddy had been there, we would've quietly giggled about kindling, salt pork, and hardtack until Mom told us to either stop or share the joke. We couldn't share the joke, of course, so we'd have to stop.

Soon we had a heaping pile of sticks in the middle of

the gravel parking area. Mom got some newspaper from the car, tucked sheets of it here and there, and lit the newspaper with a match. The paper roared into flames and burned to ashes in seconds. The sticks didn't even look warm.

"I think we need more newspaper," Mom said as she crunched two stacks of newspaper into balls and lit them. Again, no fire—just a quick-burning flame and ashes.

"Dry leaves," Rose said. "We need dry leaves."

"It was hard enough finding sticks," I said.

"I know!" Rose said. "We have to blow on it to help spread the flames. Fire needs oxygen."

Mom tucked the last of the newspaper into the pile, lit it, and Rose and I blew into the flames. It burned bright for a few seconds and then went dark.

I shook my head. "If we were pioneers, we'd be dead in two days."

"We'd make it at least one week," said Rose the rainbow-finder.

"I really wanted us to sit around the fire and eat s'mores while I read *By the Shores of Silver Lake* to you," Mom said.

"Why not *On the Banks of Plum Creek* since we're on the banks of Plum Creek?" Rose asked. "Besides, *By the Shores of Silver Lake* is one of her more depressing books."

"I didn't think about it. For some reason this is the book that called to me." Mom's shoulders slumped. "Guess it doesn't really matter. The plan isn't working anyway."

"Since when do you give up so easily?" Rose collected

the flashlights. "We can still do it. No fire. We'll just change location to the car and stay warm there."

Mom sighed, but she said, "I guess that would work."

We crammed into the back seat. Mom sat between us, using a flashlight to read the book. Rose and I ate cold s'mores, which isn't easy. They're thick, and without roasting, they don't mush together.

By the Shores of Silver Lake is sad from the beginning. Mary is blind from scarlet fever, which is obviously worse than fever 'n' ague, and on top of that, their dog is dead. Pa wants to leave Walnut Grove because the grasshoppers keep eating the crops, so he takes a job working for the railroad and moves the family to South Dakota. It's basically the Wild West, but they get to live in a nice house for a little while because of the railroad job. The house is stocked with the most food they've had since they left the big woods of Wisconsin. No more jackrabbit stew. And no more Nellie Oleson.

"Lucky Laura!" I interrupted Mom. "She finally gets rid of Nellie Oleson." I said *Nellie Oleson*, but I was thinking about Julia Ramos.

Rose said, "Here's the amazing thing. Pretty soon Laura moves to De Smet, and guess who shows up? Nellie Oleson! She tries to steal Laura's boyfriend."

"So Laura has to go to school with her again? She has to eat lunch with her and hang out at recess? Nellie is a rash that won't go away." I shivered, and it wasn't because

I was cold. I was thinking about finding a place to hide during Monday's lunch period.

"Charlotte, do you want to take over with the reading? I don't feel like it."

I took the book, but I didn't start reading because just then I got the best idea ever. "Mom, it feels like reading is getting harder and harder. School is so hard."

"But you've always had an excellent grasp of language," Mom said.

"Trust me, it's getting harder and . . . worser."

"You mean worse?"

"See!" I slapped my hand against my forehead. "I was wondering if you'd talk to the principal about me getting extra help during lunch. I can take a sandwich every day and work with Mrs. Newman. It'd really help me."

"What's going on, Charlotte?"

"Nothing. I just like Mrs. Newman, and I want to show her I can do better."

"I think you're fine just as you are." Mom patted my shoulder. "But if getting some extra help builds your confidence, then we should do it. You know your own heart and mind. I'll talk to Mrs. Newman."

"You should go straight to the principal."

"Why?"

"Mrs. Newman doesn't care about me. She says if I'm not reading well by now, it's basically too late. She wants me to focus on math."

Rose said, "You just said you like Mrs. Newman."

In addition to being a poor rainbow-finder, I was a bad liar. I spoke before I thought. I threw in details that didn't make sense. I needed my own role of duct tape. "Well, usually I like her. But not when she said that thing about reading. I didn't like her then. I like her now, though."

"She really said that?" Mom shook her head. "That's terrible. I've been feeling like something isn't right. Something is . . . off."

"Please don't say anything to the principal about her. It's a small school. I don't want to be called a troublemaker."

"All right."

"Will you call right away Monday morning? I already missed a week of school. I can't get . . . behinder."

"More behind," Mom said. "I'll call first thing."

Who's a genius?

Me, that's who.

· CHAPTER ·
EIGHT

By lunchtime Monday I was in the media center taking a reading comprehension test with the librarian.

I had to read an essay and answer questions. The essay, "Manifest Destiny and America's Expansion," was long and boring. If you've heard people say something is as boring as watching paint dry, well, the Manifest Destiny essay would bore *the paint*. I couldn't wait to get home and tell Freddy about it. Then I remembered he'd turned into Red Fred and broke our Twin Superpowers.

The essay went like this: After colonists won independence from England, American leaders thought it was destiny for our country to grow. If ordinary Americans could own land, not just rich people, then they would be committed to making the country strong and the best in the world. So the government bought land around Louisiana from France and fought with Mexico to get even more land. And pretty soon the country stretched "from sea to shining sea," just like the song "America the Beautiful" said.

The first thing I had to do was define Manifest Destiny. I wrote, *America was destiny to be from see to shiny see.*

Then I had to explain the Louisiana Purchase. *Louisiana was on sail so we bought it.*

Then I had to explain why leaders thought it was important for ordinary Americans to own land. I wrote, *????? don't understand question*

I left the rest of the questions blank and turned it in to the librarian when the dismissal bell rang.

The next day, as everyone headed to the lunchroom, Freddy stopped by my desk.

"Come to lunch with us."

"No, thanks."

"You can tell the interrupting-cow knock-knock joke."

"Not happening." In third grade, I'd heard a joke on the radio. *What's a drummer's favorite veggie? Beets.* I'd practiced it in front of the bathroom mirror; then I'd delivered it at recess to girls waiting in line for the slide. Nobody had laughed. Not even a chuckle. Amanda Perkins had rolled her eyes and said, "Beets aren't anyone's favorite vegetable."

Or was her name Amelia?

Anyway, I learned fast. No jokes.

"Come on, Charlotte. Please."

"Are your hearing aids on? Because I said no."

Freddy sighed. "Whatever." He followed the wolf pack to the cafeteria.

Mrs. Newman came over and sat in the desk next to mine. Sitting close was how she pretended to be friendly.

"I got a look at your test, Charlotte."

"Oh?"

"You definitely need to work on your reading."

I sighed. "I know."

"And you'd like to do this during lunch while the other kids are taking a break?"

"That'd be best."

"I guess that's what we'll do," she said. "For our first assignment, you'll read about the First Transcontinental Railroad. The railroad was part of the government's plan to settle the western United States."

"I'll be reading about trains? I have books from home I could—"

"What did you think you'd be reading? *Harry Potter*?"

My answer was yes, but obviously I had it wrong, so I shrugged.

She said, "The decisions we make have consequences; some of those consequences are intended and some are not intended. Perhaps reading nonfiction is an unintended consequence for you?" She looked proud of herself. "You'll have a chance to analyze the intended and unintended consequences of westward expansion. That's going to be our focus. It's all coming together beautifully, isn't it?" Mrs. Newman paused, like she was waiting for me to applaud or something, but I pressed my lips together and frowned. "I brought a book from my personal collection, and I have countless articles on homesteading laws. Do you know about homesteading laws?"

"I'm guessing they have something to do with homes and steading."

"The homesteading laws opened the West for rapid expansion. The government lured people from the relative comfort of the East by giving away free land. It was a turning point in our history. But first, more about the railroads." She handed me a heavy book titled *The First Transcontinental Railroad: The Impact of Westward Expansion on American Culture and the Economy*. If I dropped it on my foot, I'd break a toe for sure.

"One more question," Mrs. Newman said. "I read your Laura Ingalls essay, and it had tremendous qualities. Some might say it was overly negative, but I value a critical eye. And your vocabulary, syntax, and grammar? Outstanding."

Uh-oh. Big mistake. I needed to plan my lies better. I was so focused on failing the comprehension test that I didn't even think about the fact that I'd written an essay with tremendous qualities. My brain raced for an explanation as Mrs. Newman said, "If you can write an essay that's clearly above grade level, how is it that you failed a reading comprehension test?"

I had exactly one second to think about my options. If I admitted I failed the test intentionally, I'd be banished to the lunchroom and recess. So I mumbled, "I cheated."

"You cheated?"

"I copied it from the Internet."

Mrs. Newman looked suspicious. "But the essay was specific to your life. How did you find an essay online that had details about your mother's jobs and your history?"

That woman was smart. If the FBI ever needed a special agent—a very mean special agent—they could find one right here in Walnut Grove.

"Well . . ." I took a couple of breaths. "Actually, my sister wrote it. Rose. She's a genius. Just look at her school records if you don't believe me. She'll probably graduate when she's fourteen."

"So it wasn't from the Internet?"

"I just said that because I didn't want Rose to get into trouble. I . . . I told her it was an essay just for fun. I didn't tell her I needed it for class."

Mrs. Newman stared at me. "Interesting."

Students started pouring into the room, so Mrs. Newman turned and walked to her desk. I was sweating from the pressure. Mrs. Newman's eyes looked like the eyes of the lady judge on TV who was always shouting at people. She was going to dish out a horrible punishment for me in front of the whole class, but what?

Mrs. Newman stood for an announcement. "We have the results of the essay contest. Students in grades five through eight submitted essays, and I'm thrilled to say that the winner is in this class."

The class roared to life. Freckles Boy actually clapped.

I was absolutely 100 percent without-a-doubt certain the winner was Julia Ramos. She probably wrote her essay on a slate—the sort of handheld chalkboard Laura and her sister Mary shared in school. Maybe she even submitted a picture of herself in a bonnet. Julia was that kind of student.

"Congratulations to Julia Ramos!" Mrs. Newman said. See?

Julia smiled, and Tallest Girl in Class gave her a high five. I swore Freddy's brown eyes took the shape of little hearts.

"One more thing," Mrs. Newman said. "The contest was definitely close. I think it's only fair to mention the runner-up because that student did such a tremendous job."

My face went red because I knew what she was going to say before she said it.

"Congratulations, Charlotte Lake." She smiled wickedly.

Sometimes it stinks to be right.

· · · · ·

At the end of the day, when everyone left, Mrs. Newman asked me to stay for a minute. But why? She made me sweat buckets while she organized papers. I wondered if I should confess that the whole thing had started as a way to escape the lunchroom and the playground. But I knew she wouldn't understand. She'd probably lived in Walnut Grove her whole life. She didn't know what it was like to be new or to lose a twin brother.

Finally she said, "The museum folks could use more help. They don't have any money for a second student, but if you volunteer, I'll consider it your sentence for cheating. If not, I'll report it to the principal, who has zero tolerance for cheating. Do you have anything to say for yourself?"

"I made my essay negative so I *wouldn't* get the job, and—"

"You mean your sister made it negative?"

"Yes. My sister, Rose. I'm sorry. I didn't think it would turn out like this."

"Unintended consequences." Mrs. Newman stared into my eyes. "Charlotte Lake, I will not allow you to fall short of your potential."

My potential?

I didn't see that coming. I thought she'd nag me about cheating. No adult ever talked to me like that, not even Mom. When Mom talked about *potential* she meant *opening yourself to the universe.* I never thought about *potential* and *school.*

You think Mrs. Newman is one of those teacher-angels for reaching out to the quiet kid, right?

You're wrong. Mrs. Newman was ruining my Walnut Grove survival plan. She was stirring everything I wanted settled, and I didn't have Freddy to help outsmart her.

I ran to my locker. I literally ran.

· PART TWO ·

The Long, Cold, Terrible, Snowing,

Blowing Winter

NINE

The Laura Ingalls Wilder Museum smelled like someone was frying chicken strips in a thrift store. The artifacts were responsible for the musty odor, and Gloria Johnson carried the scent of the chicken strips like her own personal perfume. Outside, sleet was turning Walnut Grove into a town-sized ice rink, even though it was only November. Julia and I showed up for orientation covered in tiny ice pellets, so Gloria made hot chocolate for us while she explained the project.

In the winter, volunteers cleaned the "nooks and crannies" because the museum buildings were closed. Even the biggest Laura fans wouldn't risk prairie blizzards for a visit. But this year, in addition to the cleaning, Julia and I were going to update the catalog of artifacts. Gloria took us through the buildings and showed us how we'd take pictures of each item and log the information into a spread-sheet.

"It seems like most of the stuff here is from Walnut Grove in general, not just Laura," Julia said.

We'd been in Walnut Grove since August, and only Rose and Mom had toured the museum complex. No way would I visit the place voluntarily, and Freddy didn't have time for tours. He always hung out with the wolf pack after school. At home, Freddy talked to Mom and Rose. And I talked to Mom and Rose. But all those weeks, from the moment he'd turned into Red Fred to the first day of my prison sentence at the museum, we'd basically kept our vow of silence against each other.

"Think about it," Gloria said to Julia. "There are Laura museums in all the places she lived. Lake Pepin in Wiscon-sin, Burr Oak in Iowa, Mansfield in Missouri, De Smet in South Dakota, and a few others. We have to share her things."

"She saved everything," Julia said. "Her little handker-chiefs and old quilts and even buttons."

"Back then, it wasn't a throwaway society. You made things or bought things and you kept them and reused them. You didn't buy more and more and more and more. Just think about how many cans and bottles of soda people across the country drink in just one day. Millions in one day! And your generation complains about my generation ruining the Earth."

I rolled my eyes, but Julia actually said, "I'm sorry."

"Anyhoo, that's enough for today. Let's try to meet twice a week. Just leave a message if you aren't going to make it.

If you don't show up, and the weather's bad, I'll worry."
She chuckled. "And the weather's always bad."

．　．　．　．　．

Gloria Johnson was right. Winter had come to Walnut
Grove like a toddler having a tantrum—that's how Mom
described it—kicking and howling, without apology or
regret. And it had come early. Snow covered the grass before it had a chance to turn brown. Kids wore snow pants
under their Halloween costumes. Jack-o'-lanterns froze,
ruining the tradition of smashing them into a gooey mess.

The rare snowstorm in Lexington was nothing like your
ordinary, everyday Walnut Grove snowfall. In southwestern Minnesota, there was an unstoppable trio of snow,
wind, and cold. As soon as the plow scraped the highway
clean, wind swirled behind it and left a fresh layer of snow
and ice. The gusts could whip a few flakes into a blizzard.
Mom was so nervous about dangerous weather she wouldn't
leave the house without searching the Internet for news
about road conditions. She started chewing her fingernails.

The snow had personality. Angry pellets that scratched
your skin. Fat happy flakes. Tired wet clumps. Irritated plumes
of powder. Sometimes the snow came rapid-fire, like it was
late for an appointment; other times it seemed to float, unde-
cided about whether to land or ride the wind. Occasionally it
appeared to form on the ground and blow toward the sky.

Inside was no better. The basement was damp and cold,

so we turned on space heaters. The heaters sucked all the moisture from the air. Rose's fine hair floated above her head in a cloud of static. When we touched a door handle, we got a shock.

"I'm anxious all day about getting zapped." Mom sighed as she showed us a pair of rubber cleaning gloves. "I wear these."

"How do you type in those things?"

"It's not easy." She sighed again.

When did my mom turn into a person who sighed?

At bedtime I talked to Rose about Mom. "Observation: something's going on with Mom."

"I know." Rose turned off the space heater in our room. It was better to sleep in a chilly room than to blast the space heater all night. Otherwise we woke up with itchy skin and sometimes a bloody nose.

"I stated an observation. You're supposed to ask for evidence."

"Huh?"

"Ask me for evidence. It's not hard."

"What's wrong is the Mars book is super hard. She's going to need more time."

For a smart girl, Rose could be clueless. I said, "The evidence is she doesn't shower every day. She doesn't leave the house. She's not eating enough. I don't think Mom is a winter person."

Rose pulled a book from the shelf in the corner. "Found it." She held up Laura's book, *The Long Winter*. "She needs to read this. The entire book is about—"

"Let me guess. A long winter?"

Freddy would've laughed, but Rose just kept talking. "Mom needs to connect with Laura's winter story. It'll give her energy and creativity and happiness."

"It's like every Laura book, right? Pa gets lost in a blizzard, and they worry he's dead, but he lives."

Rose shook her head. "No. It's way worse. The winter in De Smet is one of the worst in history. The whole town almost starved and froze to death. There were hardly any trees to burn for fuel. When they ran out of coal, Laura and Pa spent every single day twisting hay into sticks for their fire, and Ma, Mary, Carrie, and Grace had nothing to do but sit around the stove and shiver."

"They should've helped twist hay sticks," I said.

Freddy would've laughed again. Not Rose. "Ma was busy grinding wheat seeds in her tiny coffee grinder. Then she'd make plain loaves of bread, and that's all they had to eat. Soon even that was down to nothing."

"Plain bread can't be worse than her turnip-and-jackrabbit stew."

Rose didn't get any of my jokes. "The guy who eventually married Laura risked his life to find wheat for the town. Finally spring came and the trains arrived with supplies. So many pioneers would've died without trains bringing stuff from the East. Trains were lifesavers."

I flopped onto my bed. "Tell that to Chinese workers. Tell that to the buffalo."

"What do you mean?"

"The railroad company hired workers from China and barely paid them and had them do all the dangerous work, like blowing up tunnels. Lots of them died. When the trains were up and running, men would sit in train cars with their guns and shoot buffalo for fun. They didn't even eat the meat. The buffalo just rotted and pretty soon buffalo became almost extinct."

"Aren't you full of sunshine and butterflies!"

"Mrs. Newman is making me read articles about pioneers and settling the West."

Rose took the lotion from the nightstand and spread it all over her arms. "It's so dry. I can't stop itching. Want some?"

"Sure." She handed me the bottle, and when our fingers touched, a shock of static electricity zapped us. I said, "No offense to Laura, but we're not winter people. Even Kentucky was too cold for Mom. She's a people person, and there aren't enough people here."

"Laura's here, and she needs Laura right now. And in the summer, Walnut Grove has a big festival for Laura. People come from all over the country. The best part is this outdoor musical. There's a spot outside of town where people sit on the hillside and watch a play about the Ingallses and the history of the town. I'm going to try out. I want to win the part of Laura."

I could see Rose, dressed in a calico dress and bonnet, churning butter at her audition. No director could refuse her.

"You really like it here, don't you?" I asked. "Better than Church Row?"

"I miss spaghetti-dinner night and the funeral-lunch ladies. But here we hang out a lot more. You and me. That's cool."

Rose was a decent sister when she wasn't acting like Miss Perfect, but she was no Freddy. "You and me," I said. "That's very cool."

No reason to hurt her feelings, right?

· · · · ·

Mrs. Newman collected our math sheets and sent everyone to the lunchroom, except for Julia and Freddy. She asked them to stay for a moment. Then she told me to get my sandwich and wait in the hall. From the tone of her voice, I could tell they were in trouble. Freddy had never been in trouble at school.

Ever since Julia had hypnotized Freddy with her hair-tossing, he'd been going to football games, hanging out with the pack after school, telling jokes in the lunchroom, and even sleeping over at Spiked Hair Boy's house. And now there was trouble at school.

Thanks for nothing, Julia Ramos.

I rushed to my locker, grabbed my lunch, and went back to the classroom. I leaned against the door and strained to hear them talking. I couldn't make out Julia's words, but Mrs. Newman never had a problem being heard.

"It's disruptive and rude. You can visit in the lunchroom or outside. You can talk before and after school. I won't tolerate this note passing. This is the second time I've had to confront you. It better be the last."

Mrs. Newman should leave teaching and go to the police academy. Even I hadn't noticed the note passing, and I noticed everything.

"Sorry," Freddy mumbled.

I backed up a few feet and stood by the drinking fountain until Freddy and Julia walked toward the lunchroom. Then I sat next to Mrs. Newman's desk with my lunch and the articles she'd given me.

"I see by the smile on your face that you overheard us."

I felt my face turn red. "No. Not at all. I'm smiling because I liked the article very much."

"You're not a skilled liar, Charlotte." At first I thought she was cracking a joke, but Mrs. Newman never joked, so I cleared my throat and said, "I was fascinated by the article about the Fence Cutting Wars."

Mrs. Newman's brown curls looked extra tight. "Enlighten me."

"Well, barbed wire was a new invention in the 1800s. Those sharp points on the wires kept people and animals from going through the fence. So ranchers started fencing up big sections of land, but other people thought it should be open for travel and cattle grazing and all that. A drought made it even worse because the fences made it harder to get to water. People would cut the fences. Everybody was fighting over land and water."

"How does this relate to homesteading?" she asked.

"People kept moving west to get free land, and nobody really thought much about things like who could put up fences and who could block the way to rivers and lakes. The government didn't plan for conflict between farmers who wanted to plant crops and ranchers who wanted the land for the cattle."

"Excellent. All this reading ties nicely into your work at the museum."

I didn't make the connection. "Was Pa Ingalls a fence cutter?"

"No." She laughed. It might have been the first time I'd seen all her teeth. "But the Ingallses were part of the era and the conflict over land." She handed me an article. "I need to meet with Mr. Crenski for a few minutes. You can eat your lunch and read this."

The title of the article: "Prairie Madness." I skimmed it quickly and saw the words *pioneers, prairie, depression*, and *insanity*. I stopped skimming and started reading.

Homesteading laws brought a wave of pioneers eager to own land in the West and make their fortune. They left the relative comfort of the East and discovered they were un-prepared for the harsh life and isolation.

Settlers spread out, making it difficult to socialize. News of the outside world came sporadically. Visiting family back East was a near impossibility. Medical care was scarce, and sick children often died. Settlers worked from dawn to dusk and lived in a constant state of exhaustion.

Sometimes they went hungry. They were unprepared for weather—heat and storms in the summer; blizzards in the winter. The howling prairie winds drove people mad. Violence, alcoholism, and suicide . . .

I put the article into my desk because I had to go to the bathroom.

A few steps down the hall I skidded to a stop.

You know the moment when you learn about something totally general, something totally random, and then suddenly it's not general or random *at all*? Suddenly it's very real and very specific?

At that moment, it came to me. Prairie Madness wasn't a school lesson. It had a name and a face. Martha Lake. My mother.

Okay, the howling prairie winds hadn't exactly driven her to alcohol or violence or suicide. She'd been driven to sighing and napping and not washing her hair. Big difference.

Still, I worried. She wasn't herself.

We moved all the time. Our world was always changing, but the one thing I could count on was Martha Lake being the same rainbow-finding, energy-connecting, peace-loving mother. Not now. She didn't even leave the basement most days. She was acting like an early prairie pioneer—lonely, exhausted, sad.

Prairie Madness sounded worse than fever 'n' ague.

Way worse.

TEN

Before I went to the museum, I walked home to get a snack. Mom was sitting in the recliner with her laptop and a thick quilt wrapped around her.

I wanted to make her laugh, so I said, "Mom, do you have fever 'n' ague?"

"I'm cold because I turned off the space heaters. It's so dry I got a bloody nose."

She didn't get the joke at all, so I tried a different approach: supporting and interested daughter.

"How's the Mars book?"

"It's coming along. Aren't you supposed to be at the museum?"

"I'm on my way." Mom didn't know I'd been arm-twisted

into volunteering. I'd made it sound like I was interested in community service and devoted to Laura.

Rose popped out of our bedroom. "Can I come? Please?"

"Take her," Mom said. "You two should get out of this basement as much as possible."

Lately Rose wanted to do everything with me, and I was getting tired of her. But I could avoid talking to Julia if Rose came. I decided to test Mom for Prairie Madness. "I'll take her if you come, too, Mom. You need to get out of the basement more than anyone. And you can surround yourself with Laura's buttons and handkerchiefs."

"I'm working."

The words tumbled out of me. "You don't socialize. You work from dawn to dusk, hearing nothing but the howling prairie winds!"

"You should get out, Mom. It'll be fun," Rose said.

Mom sighed. "I am getting out. I promise. This weekend I'm going to a writing seminar in Minneapolis and staying at a hotel. Mia will keep an eye on you. I shouldn't spend the money, but I desperately need a creative jump start."

"But connecting with Laura is free," Rose said.

I glared at Rose. "That's awesome, Mom. Do you want me to put some lavender oil in the diffuser before we leave? It'll be relaxing, and it'll smell really nice."

She shook her head.

No lavender oil? No connecting with Laura?

Prairie Madness wasn't history. It was alive and well in modern-day Walnut Grove.

• • • • •

Julia and Rose chatted while they cleaned display cases near the museum's entrance. I wanted to avoid Julia, so I washed the cases on the other side of the room. Against the wall were rows of shelves displaying photos of actors from the *Little House on the Prairie* television show. Mom had watched the show when she was a kid, but I'd never seen it. I looked at the picture of actor Michael Landon, who played Pa Ingalls. He had a smooth face, dark hair that swooped along his jawline, and a smile from a toothpaste commercial.

I walked to the next case and looked at the photo of the real Pa Ingalls. Old-fashioned photos are always weird, because they're black-and-white and the people in them never smile. But Pa Ingalls was downright scary. His eyes were empty, like the eyes of a zombie, and his thick beard looked like a baby porcupine was squatting on his chin.

Creepy, right?

Julia scooted toward me. "Are you getting paid, too?"

"I'm volunteering because it's a nice thing to do." No way would I tell her I was being punished for cheating, or that I'd pretended to cheat. Julia probably couldn't keep a secret.

Gloria and Teresa, another volunteer, studied the cases from every possible angle and used a flashlight to make sure every streak had been removed. Even Ma Ingalls wasn't that fussy, and she swept dirt floors. While they checked our work, I inspected the artifacts on the walls and in the cases—some props from the television show but mostly items donated from people in southwestern Minnesota. Bonnets, button-up shoes, handmade suspenders, a man's shaving kit, a hand mirror, quilts, baby gowns. I touched the old sewing machine and wondered how many shirts, pants, and dresses had been stitched by its needle.

"You really should open in the winter," Rose said.

"Even if the weather wasn't terrible, kids are in school. Families can't visit," Teresa said.

"There's so much to see." Rose spun around. "Millions and millions of people will never see this amazing place and all these things".

Gloria nodded. "It breaks my heart that we can't share it with the whole world."

"If only there was a way to transport people here," Teresa said.

What century did these ladies live in? They probably still talked on telephones with cords.

"There is a way," I said. "As long as we're taking photos of every item for the museum records, why don't we put some of the pictures online? Imagine a museum scrapbook that anyone with a computer can see."

The room was so quiet I could hear the sleet tapping against the building. Finally Gloria said, "I'm not an Interneter. Is that even possible?"

"Of course!" Rose said.

"But how?"

Julia looked like she was going to offer an idea, but I jumped in first. "The museum already has a website. We could create new pages for the scrapbook, then upload the photos and type in descriptions." Gloria and Teresa looked at me like I'd just announced a cure for cancer. "Who does the website now?" I asked.

"My daughter's friend's niece," Gloria said. "How much would all this cost?"

"Probably not much. Maybe nothing."

Teresa beamed. "That's brilliant."

I shrugged like, *hey, no big deal*, but my heart swelled.

Gloria bubbled with happiness. "See, your family landed in Walnut Grove for a reason. You belong here. It was meant to be."

"Destiny," Rose said.

"God's plan," Teresa said.

I waited for Julia to make a nasty Nellie Oleson comment, but she smiled and said, "Good idea, Charlotte." She must have had some scheme in the works and was just playing nice. Good thing I knew who she really was.

I let Julia and Rose run ahead as we went home. The sleet had stopped, and the clouds had split apart and vanished. It felt good to walk in the cool air. I'd one-upped Julia with my idea, but I wasn't thinking about being better than Julia. That didn't even matter. I was thinking about Gloria saying we belonged in Walnut Grove. I'd never been part of anything bigger than my family. In Lexington we went to funerals, but that was just for the free lunch. I told myself that it was stupid to think about belonging here or anywhere. I reminded myself of Molly Smith and the letter that never came.

But walking under the clear blue sky, their words of praise ringing in my ears, I felt good. I felt better than good, actually. I felt . . . what did Teresa say? Brilliant. I felt brilliant. I was a girl with a brilliant idea, and I'd actually said it out loud. Me. Charlotte Lake, invisible girl.

Who knew?

. . . . .

My happiness flipped upside down when I got home. Mom had talked to Mia and come up with the worst possible plan. This Saturday while Mom was at her overnight writing conference, Freddy and Julia had permission to invite friends over to hang out in the basement. Mia and Miguel would be upstairs to supervise. Mom was convinced that if I just opened myself to the universe, anything was possible.

"Anything?" I asked.

"Anything," she said. I was sorry I'd ever thought about blue skies and brilliance. Posting pictures on the Internet was one thing. Hanging out with Freddy and Julia was another.

"Is it possible Miguel and Mia will let me go upstairs and watch a movie with them?"

Mom put her hands on my face and looked into my

eyes. "Charlotte, have fun with your friends. Enjoy your youth before you outgrow it."

I started to say, "They're not my friends," but Mom was already packing her computer, notebook, and pens into a canvas bag. My stomach clenched, and I knew it was a lost cause.

It'd been weeks now, and the wolf pack hadn't turned on Freddy. Once I'd seen a news story about this man who raised a wolf puppy, and the wolf acted like a loyal dog for years, and then one day, for no reason at all, it attacked the guy. A doctor had to amputate the man's hand. School was basically a big wolf den. The longer this fake-nice stuff went on, the more it would hurt Freddy when the wolf-friends bit him.

And when Julia stopped tossing her hair and started saying mean things, Freddy would be crushed. How long would it take for Freddy to find out Julia wasn't the girl he thought she was?

On Saturday, the door opened and a tangle of legs careened down the steps. Julia, Spiked Hair Boy, Purple Glasses Girl, Boy Who Needs Braces, and Red Fred, who'd been waiting upstairs for everyone to arrive.

I slipped into my bedroom before anyone saw me. I grabbed the handle to shut the door and was zapped by the static electricity. Then I realized I'd left my *Hunger Games* books on the table. Since I had nothing else to do, I decided to read the most recent article from Mrs. Newman. While the wolf pack talked and laughed outside my door, I read about the Dust Bowl, which is not an actual bowl of dust, but an area of the country covered in dust because all the healthy soil had been stripped away.

When the government lured settlers west with offers of free land, they weren't always honest about the type of land. So people ended up moving to desolate places that weren't good for farming, like parts of Oklahoma and Texas. The government got people to grow wheat on soil that was best used for buffalo grazing. So those people farmed and farmed, and when a big drought hit, the buffalo grasses were gone—grasses that would've held the dirt in place. When the winds came in the 1930s, they churned dirt into storms that looked like black tidal waves sweeping across the land. People died from pneumonia because of dust in their lungs. Animals died. Crops died. Houses were practically buried in dirt. The sky refused to rain.

And it happened during the Depression when Americans already didn't have jobs or money or good food. They had dirt, an ocean of dirt. These weren't just unintended consequences of homesteading; they were *depressing* unintended consequences. I wondered if Mrs. Newman ever did anything fun, or if she just sat at her computer and Googled "ways to make Charlotte feel bad."

A chorus of laughter came from the living room. Freddy's laugh was the loudest. Then I heard Rose laugh and say, "No way!" Those kids were so fake-nice they were even including a younger kid in their fun. I stretched on my bed and stared at the ceiling. I was hungry and thirsty and bored. I was sick of reading about dust.

More laughter.

What was so funny?

I figured I should check it out in case they were laughing *at* Rose, and she didn't understand that she was the butt of the joke. Sure, Rose was smart, but she was only eleven. I couldn't expect her to face a wolf pack alone.

Everyone was sitting in a circle on the floor. Boy Who Needs Braces chugged a glass of water while everyone laughed. Rose said, "Hi, Charlotte!" and all eyes landed on me. I had to say something.

"What's going on?"

Julia could hardly breathe she was laughing so hard. "Truth or Dare. Chuck had to eat a tablespoon of plain mustard."

"You're lucky I didn't puke on your shoes." Boy Who Needs Braces took a fistful of potato chips and packed them into his mouth. He blew crumbs as he talked. "Anything to get rid of the taste!"

Rose said, "Can I ask this time?"

"Sure," Freddy said.

"Okay. Bao. Truth or dare?"

"Truth."

"Who's the cutest boy in school?"

Purple Glasses Girl slapped her hands over her face. "Nobody!"

"Truth!" Rose shouted. "You have to pick somebody."

Purple Glasses Girl smiled and sat up straight. "Liam."

"Who's that?" Freddy asked.

"He's the cutest little kindergartner I've ever seen."

"Cheater!" Rose laughed. "Next time I'm going to be specific and say pick someone from your class."

"Thanks for the warning. I'll make sure I don't pick truth again. Now I get to pick somebody. Charlotte."

I froze. I thought about saying no thanks and blaming a headache. But maybe if I played I'd get a nickname and I'd get invited to parties? Did I want a nickname? Maybe. Did I want to get invited to parties? Maybe. Did I want to laugh on Friday nights with other kids? Maybe. Did I want friends who'd disappear like Molly Smith? No. Did I want friends to make promises and then break them like Molly Smith? No.

I studied the faces of Spiked Hair Boy, Boy Who Needs Braces, and Purple Glasses Girl, and they weren't frowning or rolling their eyes or staring at me like I was an alien. They were just waiting for an answer.

You know what happened next?

Freddy said, "Charlotte, pick. Truth or dare."

"Dare." The word just slipped out.

Purple Glasses Girl said, "I dare to you to get a pen and draw a mustache on Rose."

Everyone laughed. Rose protested, but I could tell she was thrilled to be included in the dare. I swallowed hard and tried to think of an escape, but Freddy tossed me a pen. I caught it and knelt next to Rose. With a shaking hand, I drew a thick mustache on her face. Purple

Glasses Girl took a picture with her phone. When Rose saw it she squealed with delight.

"Now you pick someone," Rose told me. "That's how the game works."

My heart pumped. Who should I pick? I couldn't pick one of the boys because they might think I liked them, and I mean the weird kind of like. Julia was the safe bet, but what if she said truth? What would I ask? What if she said dare? I'd have to think of something clever. I considered the headache plan again, but everyone was smiling at me and they did seem like they were having fun. Finally I said, "Julia."

"Dare!"

I sat down next to Rose. "Let me think. Um . . . I dare you to act like a gorilla for thirty seconds."

Julia jumped around, made monkey noises, and pretended to pick bugs out of Freddy's hair and eat them, which got a big laugh. Freddy laughed, too. He wasn't acting like a beige chair against a beige wall. He was one hundred percent Red Fred. Without saying anything, I sat down on the floor next to Rose. And just like that, I was part of the circle.

We played a few more rounds of Truth or Dare, then stopped to eat. Freddy cut the pizzas and gave Julia the first piece, which also happened to be the biggest piece. He opened a bag of Oreos and doled them out evenly, but there was one extra, which he put on Julia's plate.

Spiked Hair Boy said, "Remember last summer when we played flashlight tag in the park? It's not very cold. Want to do that?"

Heads nodded, but Julia said, "No. Bad Chad. He'll be out there waiting for someone to torture."

Rose said, "Freddy has a game on our phone called What's the Word? You hold the phone so you can't see it, and a word appears on the screen, and your teammate has to give you clues to guess what the word is. Whichever teams gets the most number of words in a minute wins."

Everyone thought that sounded fun. Rose announced she would divide us into teams, and Freddy said, "You can put me with Julia if nobody else wants to be on her team." Rose selected Bao for her team. I was paired with Spiked Hair Boy—Noah—which made me nervous, because . . . I don't know. Just because.

It took Freddy thirty seconds to guess *spider* despite Julia giving obvious clues, but Noah and I made a good team. We got the hardest words and nailed them. We only had a few seconds left when Noah's eyes popped open at the next word, like it'd be a miracle if I guessed it.

Noah: "What's the word for something that's like a deer only—"

Me: "Elk!"

Noah: "Like an elk and a deer but . . . poetic."

Me: "Gazelle?"

Noah: "Yessssss!"

The phone beeped, and our turn was over.

Julia and Freddy shook their heads in disbelief. "How'd you get that?" Freddy asked. "What's a gazelle?"

"Like a deer," Noah said.

"Or an elk," I said.

"Only poetic," we said at the same time. Noah high-fived me.

Then Miguel came downstairs. "Time to call it a night. I'll drive you kids home." His accent was heavier than Mia's. Sometimes I'd hear them speaking Spanish, but Julia never said a word in Spanish, not even *hola*.

"Fifteen more minutes?" Julia asked.

"Parents are expecting kids home, and I'm ready to go to bed."

There were groans and grumbling, but everyone put on their winter gear and headed upstairs.

What's the word for better-than-I-thought-it-would-be? *Okay*.

It was *okay*.

I'd say *fun*, but let's not get ahead of ourselves, right?

ELEVEN

I got to school Monday just before the bell rang. As Noah walked past my locker, I started to say hello, but he shouted, "Gazelle!" and laughed and walked into class. I tapped Bao's shoulder.

"That was a joke, right?"

"Of course." She laughed like there was no doubt.

At lunchtime, I reached in my backpack and realized I had left my lunch on the counter at home. Mom had come back from the conference with a bad cold, so she'd overslept, which meant all of us had overslept. Then I discovered all my jeans were in the laundry, so I had to do the sniff test to see which pair was wearable, then I couldn't find my gloves. I only had a few bites of toast before stuffing my books into my backpack. I had rushed outside without my sandwich, banana, and crackers.

Everyone else headed to the lunchroom, but I sat at my desk looking through my stack of articles. I had one on the Gold Rush, one on the Oregon Trail, one on Oklahoma migrants moving to California, and one on the Interstate Highway System.

Mrs. Newman came and stood over my desk. "Did you read the article about the Dakota Sioux Conflict?"

"Sorry, but I was busy this weekend. My mom was gone, so I kind of had to watch my sister."

Mrs. Newman raised her eyebrow. "Kind of had to?"

"Definitely had to."

"I want you to start with the Dakota Sioux Conflict because it was essentially a war that happened right here in southwestern Minnesota. The whole thing was over-shadowed by the Civil War, so most people know very little about it. You'll make some connections between it and the Ingalls family."

"Like Ma hating Indians?"

"In a way," she said. "No doubt she'd heard about Indians killing settlers in southwestern Minnesota, and she was afraid."

"It's not like she could call 911."

"Indians were afraid of the settlers, too. The government broke treaty after treaty. They didn't give the Indians supplies that were promised, and the Indians were afraid they'd starve that winter." Mrs. Newman noticed I wasn't eating. "Where's your lunch?"

"I kind of forgot my lunch at home."

She put her hands on her hips. "It doesn't sound like you 'kind of' forgot your lunch. It sounds like you 'definitely' forgot your lunch."

"I guess."

"Then you need to go to the lunchroom and eat." She didn't even fake smile, so I knew there was no way around it.

Even though my heart pounded, I went to the lunchroom. Nearly everyone was through the line, so I quickly collected a taco, rice, green beans, peaches, and milk. I looked around for Freddy or Julia or Bao.

"Charlotte! Charlotte!"

Bao waved me over to her table and scooted closer to Obviously Popular Girl. I could see the back of Freddy at the next table, talking to Big Nose Boy and Chue aka Chuck. Julia was sitting at the end of our table next to Emma.

"How come you're at lunch today?" Bao asked.

"I forgot my lunch at home."

Tallest Girl in Class said, "Red Fred says you don't need special reading help. Why do you stay in class?"

I shrugged. "I just like to read."

"Me, too," Emma said. "But I'd never stay in class to do it. What are you reading in there?"

I thought about lying and saying *Harry Potter*. But if

they'd seen the Transcontinental Railroad book or the articles about Fence Cutters, it'd be worse. It'd look like I was hiding my secret love of trains and fences. In kindergarten I'd made the mistake of admitting I liked Thomas the Train, and three girls yelled "Choo choo!" in my face.

How did Freddy figure out these lunchroom conversations?

"I'm reading about stuff like homesteading and the Oregon Trail and the Interstate Highway System. Did you know we had an entire war with Mexico over who got to own Texas?" I realized I was acting a little too excited, so I dialed it back. "I guess Mrs. Newman thinks all this stuff will help me at the museum."

"What do highways have to do with Laura?" Bao asked.

"Building the highway was just another way to connect the East with the West."

Bao said, "I don't see how that helps with the project at the museum."

Mrs. Newman would want me to tell them about westward expansion through time and the intended and unintended consequences, but I wasn't crazy. That would be like teasing wolves with raw meat. Julia would probably be the first one to bite. "Who knows? Mrs. Newman has weird ideas."

"Really weird," Bao said.

"Really, really weird," Emma said.

They started talking about homework, so I just

nodded while I studied the cafeteria. Freddy was a Walnut Grove superstar. Evidence? Big Nose Boy was wearing a Bruce Springsteen T-shirt with an unzipped hoodie. Curly Hair Girl was wearing a Nirvana T-shirt with an unzipped hoodie. Freckles Boy? Rolling Stones with an unzipped hoodie. I bet he didn't even know a single Rolling Stones song. Red Fred had started a fashion trend. Mom always bought his shirts at thrift stores, and most of them were old rock-and-roll shirts, and he always added a hoodie.

When it was time to go outside, I slipped into the bathroom and waited until the bell rang to go back to class. No need to take chances. I'd been lucky, and lunch had gone fine, but I couldn't risk the playground, too. Sad fact: luck runs out.

. . . . .

When I got to the museum, Julia, Rose, Gloria, and Teresa were eating brownies in the break room. Gloria served me a brownie. "Teresa brought some of her homemade chicken soup. It's in the refrigerator. You can bring it home for your mother."

"I heard she's feeling blue," Teresa said. "We can't have our celebrity author sick when she's writing about the prairie. We need her to do us proud."

How'd they know about Mom's Prairie Madness? I wondered if Mom had talked to Mia and Mia had talked to

Miguel and Miguel had talked to Julia who spread it all over town.

"Her book will be great for the museum, for the festival, for the entire town," Gloria said. "Imagine having another bestselling book set in Walnut Grove. Laura Ingalls did an injustice when she wrote *On the Banks of Plum Creek* because she never named the town. I'm not kidding. You will not find the words Walnut Grove anywhere in that book. In the television show, yes. The book? No. Such a shame."

Apparently Laura hadn't considered unintended consequences of not naming the town—museum ladies 150 years later would hold a grudge.

"Then they went and filmed the television show in *California*! What a joke!" Teresa wrinkled her nose.

"Maybe someday we'll have a new museum building for your mother." Gloria licked the chocolate frosting off her finger. "Maybe the Ramos home will be part of a tour!"

"How cool would that be!" Julia practically gasped. "I think this is going to be my favorite year ever."

Obviously Mom had not told anyone outside our family about Mars, because if she had, Teresa and Gloria would know. Somehow they'd know. They'd hear it from Shorty at the gas station or the guy who runs the Asian grocery or somebody's brother's cousin's uncle's wife. Suddenly the brownie lost its flavor. Rose said, "Thank you for the soup. I know she'll appreciate it."

"You bet," Teresa said.

"If Teresa's soup doesn't make her better, then she should see a doctor." Gloria winked at Teresa.

"Why?" Julia asked. "What's in it?"

"It's my grandmother's recipe. The secret is chicken gizzards."

I was afraid to ask, but I did. "What's a gizzard?"

"It's part of the stomach," Teresa said. "I know, I know. You kids have only seen boneless skinless chicken breasts looking all pretty in a plastic wrapper."

Julia said, "My grandma makes whole chickens."

"You're the exception," Gloria said. "The old-timers ate organ meat from animals all the time—liver, kidney, gizzards. That's why sixty-year-old farmers could still work the land twelve hours a day. They were strong from all that iron and protein."

Teresa nodded. "I read that blueberries and spinach are power foods. Hah! Cow tongue. That's a power food. My mom used to make it, and I still have her recipe."

"Cow tongue? Really?" Rose wrinkled her nose. "I don't think the Ingallses ate cow tongue. Laura and Mary ate pig's tail, but it probably tastes like bacon. What does cow tongue taste like?"

"How can I describe cow tongue?" Teresa closed her eyes for a moment, searching for words. "It's incredibly tender. It's like butter that tastes like meat."

"My father's favorite was liver and onions," Gloria said. "It kept him strong. He worked a plow until he was seventy. He had a lot of problems—I'll just say he enjoyed certain beverages and you can fill in the blanks—but age was not one of them."

I thought about the chicken strips at the Prairie Diner and hoped they'd come from a box and not an old-timer's recipe.

Gloria put the cover on the pan of brownies. "Let's get to work."

. . . . .

When we got home, Mom was wrapped in a blanket with her computer on her lap. Her hair hung around her face in greasy strands, and her feet were tucked into mismatched slippers. She stared at the screen. Didn't type. Just stared. Our breakfast dishes were still scattered on the kitchen table.

"Is it sunny outside?" she asked without looking at us.

"Not today," Rose said. "But guess what? We have gizzard soup for you."

Mom made a face. "Lizard soup?"

"Gizzard, as in chicken neck or chicken stomach or whatever," I said. "It's pretty much like chicken noodle soup. I'll warm up a bowl for you."

"Thanks, honey, but I'm not hungry."

I beckoned Rose into the bedroom and quietly said, "Observation: Mom needs an intervention."

"There's a bright side. Sure, she's not getting out, and

she's not acting totally normal, but it's because she's working hard. The harder she works, the better the book will be. I know it looks bad, but it's actually good."

How were we even related? Rose was going to be no help with Mom.

But Freddy had figured out the wolf pack. He knew how to observe evidence. Maybe he'd have an idea about Mom. I had to do something, and so I did it fast, before I changed my mind. I went to Freddy's room and knocked on the door.

"Charlotte?" He blinked in surprise.

"Obviously."

He sat on his bed, and I closed the door behind me.

"We need to talk about something," I said.

Then our phone chirped with a text. As he typed an answer, Rose pushed her way into his room. "You're mean!"

I couldn't agree more, but I didn't think accusing Freddy of being mean was the way to get him to help with Mom. But when I turned to Rose, she wasn't looking at Freddy. You'll never guess who she was glaring at.

Me!

"Why am I the mean one? Freddy's mean. He's texting while I'm trying to talk to him."

"You walked out in the middle of a conversation." Rose crossed her arms.

"I was texting before you got here," Freddy said. "Technically you're interrupting me. You're both interrupting me."

Rose's face burned red. "See how Freddy acts? I'm the one talking to you and being nice to you. And you still just want to talk to him!"

Those were not rainbow words. Both Freddy and I stared at Rose. Her eyes darted back and forth like she was watching people play ping-pong. The phone in Freddy's hand dinged once, twice, three times. He couldn't keep his eyes off the screen.

"Just forget it," I said. "I'm going to bed." And as Freddy stared at the phone and Rose stared at me, I walked out of the room, put on my pajamas, and crawled into bed. I didn't even say good night to Mom or brush my teeth.

Sleep didn't come, though. I tossed and turned, fuming about Freddy's texting addiction, steaming about Rose's stupid accusations, until I decided to get up. I went to the kitchen for some water and crackers. The basement was dark. Mom and Rose had gone to bed. But Mom's laptop was on the kitchen table. Without thinking, I opened it and looked at the websites she had open in her browser. One tab was the *New York Times* bestseller list for children's books, which made sense. Someone writing a book for kids would study the list. The other page was Secrets of Bestselling Novels, which also made sense.

Then I looked through her documents. She had four folders: short stories, essays, nonfiction, novels. I clicked on novels. Inside that folder were two files: Prairie.doc and Mars.doc. I opened the Mars file.

Page one said, *Untitled Mars Novel.*

Page two said, *Chapter One.*

That was it. Two pages; five words.

We'd come to Walnut Grove three months ago so Mom could write her novel, and her fingers had barely touched the keyboard. Five words! Rose wouldn't be able to find a rainbow here, Freddy abandoned me, and Mom had Prairie Madness.

What was next? Grasshoppers dropping from the sky? An outbreak of fever 'n' ague? Blindness?

Walnut Grove was cursed.

TWELVE

When the lunch bell rang the next day, Bao tapped me on the shoulder. "You're coming to lunch, right?"

I had the Dust Bowl article in my backpack. I'd even read a second article about hungry migrants leaving Oklahoma and heading west for jobs. Plus I'd brought my favorite lunch—leftover pizza—and my nose told me a stomach-churning tuna fish casserole would greet us in the cafeteria.

So you know what I said?

"Sure."

I don't know how it happened. I meant to say no. I meant to say no while shaking my head so there'd be no doubt. But my mouth had other ideas.

"Sure." My mouth said it *again*. "Mrs. Newman, is it

okay if I have lunch in the cafeteria? I forgot my lunch at home again."

"That's fine. Give us a minute, Bao."

Bao left the classroom with everyone else, and I went to Mrs. Newman's desk.

"Charlotte, if everything goes well today, is there a chance you'll forget your lunch at home again?"

I felt my face turn red. "Maybe."

"Your reading seems to have improved dramatically. How does it seem to you?"

"Better."

"I think we can be done with these sessions. Enjoy your lunch."

My heart pounded at the thought. I cleared my throat. "Mrs. Newman?"

"Yes?"

"What if today is fine, but tomorrow is a disaster?"

"Let's assume it's going to go well. And if it doesn't, we'll come up with a plan." She handed me an article. I glanced at the title—something about Native Americans and a Trail of Tears. "Here's one more thing I want you to read. You can take your time, but I do want to discuss it."

I left the article on my desk and went to the cafeteria. When I sat down next to Bao, Julia was already telling her about the gizzard soup. Then Emma talked about her grandma's liver and onions, and Bao said something about her grandma using fish oil in soup, and suddenly it seemed like it was my turn to say something. I couldn't think of any weird food stories. I felt nervous and empty, but then I had an idea.

"What are you going to do with your museum money, Julia?"

Julia talked about a bike and new clothes. Bao and Emma tossed out ideas for Julia's wish list, and I added things like *The Hunger Games* DVD set and a Hermione Granger wand. My idea worked! I came up with a new observation: if you don't have clever stories or jokes, then ask questions. I wondered if Freddy had noticed the same evidence. Maybe that's how he'd survived the week I was sick.

Before I had a chance to start feeling sad about Freddy, the bell rang. Everyone's food was gone, including mine. Lunch had passed in a blink.

Stupid bell.

. . . . .

As winter descended, the world got colder and darker, but I felt warmer and brighter. I saw rainbows everywhere—in the lunchroom, in the classroom, in the museum.

Lunches went by in a blink. There were so many things to say I barely had time to eat my tater tot hot dish.

Bao and Emma weren't fake-nice; they were nice-nice. Sometimes we laughed so hard my stomach hurt.

I made sure to do my homework every night, and it came back with notes from Mrs. Newman that said *Excellent!* and *Outstanding!*

And the most surprising rainbow: Julia Ramos started acting less like Nellie Oleson. Working at the museum with her wasn't horrible. It was okay.

I'd say fun, but let's not start exaggerating, right?

I tried to bring my rainbow attitude home, but it wasn't contagious. Rose found out she wasn't going to Greece with her dad for Christmas. She cried for two hours, and Mom didn't change out of her pajamas for three days. The Mars book still had only five words on two pages.

Everything about Freddy was contagious, though. When he broke a shoelace, Mom found a stray purple shoelace in a drawer. Freddy went to school with a black shoelace on his right shoe and a purple one on his left. Soon nearly everyone in class was wearing different-colored shoelaces. Not me, of course. Freddy and I were talking again, but it wasn't Twin Superpowers talk. It was pass-the-salt, give-me-the-remote kind of talk. Definitely no laughs. He spent most of his time in his room while Rose followed me around the basement.

A week before Christmas break, Julia and I were ready to show Gloria and Teresa sample pages of the scrapbook. We gathered around the computer, and in a few clicks I pulled up a page of farm equipment and tools used in the late 1800s. Together we'd written descriptions of how the items were used. I had to admit it: Julia worked hard, she always gave me credit for what I did, and she had good ideas of her own.

"Here's a page of tools," I said.

"Goodness!" Gloria said. "Is it on the website now?"

"Not yet. This is just a template," I said. "We want to finish the whole scrapbook before we publish it online. We still have to figure out the technical stuff."

Julia cleared her throat. "I have an idea, too, if you want to hear it."

"Sure."

"This is for down the road. You know, like phase two. I've been thinking we could tape interviews with the oldest people in town about their memories, and we could upload the videos, too."

"Goodness!" Gloria said again.

"You are simply amazing." Teresa patted Julia's shoulder. "I never even thought this was possible."

For a second I felt annoyed, maybe even a little jealous. Then I saw the smile flash on Julia's face, and I remembered how I felt that day I walked home from the museum, the day Teresa said I was brilliant. I knew exactly how Julia was feeling, and I wasn't going to take it away from her.

"That's a good idea, Julia," I said.

I even meant it, you know?

While we finished up, I got an idea. Maybe it was a terrible idea. But maybe it wasn't. Maybe, in fact, it was a good idea. Maybe I was finding a rainbow.

As Julia and I walked home from the museum, I asked a question.

"Julia, do you have a lot of homework?"

"No. Why?"

Then I blurted out my idea and braced myself for her answer. "Do you want to walk to the diner and have hot chocolate?"

She smiled. "Awesome. Let's do it."

． ． ． ． ．

"It cracks me up every time Gloria says, 'I'm not an Interneter.'" Julia blew on her hot chocolate before taking a sip. "Did you hear Teresa say, 'Can we send this on *the* email?'"

"And Gloria asked about putting it on *the* Facebook," I said. "They're hilarious."

"Seriously, Charlotte, the scrapbook is a great idea."

"Thanks. The video is even better. Some of those tools are so weird looking, you can't even imagine what they were used for. It'd be cool if someone could do a quick demonstration of how they were used."

"If the tools don't fall apart." Julia gulped. "Gloria and Teresa would have heart attacks!"

"We'd get fired."

"Arrested."

"Jailed for life."

We both laughed. Julia said, "People can just talk in the videos. No demonstrations. We'll stick with your original scrapbook plan for the tools."

Then it was quiet, and I wasn't sure what to say, but I remembered the trick from lunch: ask questions.

"So what are you doing for Christmas?"

Julia wrinkled her nose. "Seeing my dad. Do you see your dad at Christmas?"

Freddy and I didn't talk about our dad to other people. How do you explain that your dad wasn't the man your mom thought he was and that your sister has an entirely different father? And that he wasn't the man your mom thought he was, either? You don't. And why was Julia so interested anyway? Julia's nose-wrinkling thing let me flip the conversation back to her. "You don't seem happy about seeing yours."

"I'm not. But there's a judge who makes sure he gets to see me. He has to visit at my grandparents' though. We don't go anywhere. It's weird. He just asks me questions about school, and then we watch TV. I hate being in a room with him."

"Why?"

Julia looked down at her hot chocolate. I waited. I wished I could take back asking why, but it was too late. Rose loves seeing her dad, so I didn't understand why Julia would hate being in the same room as hers.

Finally Julia leaned closer and spoke quietly. "My dad robbed Shorty's gas station. So I don't usually tell people when he's here. Don't tell anyone he's visiting, okay? He drives a different car now."

My eyes opened wide. "Your dad robbed a gas station?"

"I can't believe you didn't already know. Everybody knows. It was the night my mom dumped him. She's doing good now. She got cleaned up, and she even got a scholarship. And when she's done with school in Chicago, she'll move back and I'll live with her again." Julia looked so proud. "Just promise you won't say anything about my dad visiting."

I'd never been asked to keep a secret before. Freddy and I had our Twin Superpowers, so we always talked about everything. That's how it used to be. But the secret with Julia was different. She didn't have to tell me about her dad, but she did. It was a secret for friends.

"I won't tell. Promise." I wanted Julia to feel better, so I said, "Maybe we've spent too much time in the museum, but it seems like Walnut Grove has an image of the perfect dad, and it's Pa Ingalls." I wrinkled my nose in support. "The perfect fiddle-playing dad."

Julia snorted. "Mr. Hard Work."

"Mr. Church Bell Donor."

"Right? He finally gets some money from that farming job, and instead of buying his kids shoes or bonnets, he buys a bell for the church."

"Did you write about Pa in your essay?" I asked.

"I wrote about Walnut Grove and the Hmong immigrants."

"What's Hmong? "

"The Asians here are Hmong, which is like Vietnamese, but not exactly. Tons of them came to Minnesota after the war in Vietnam."

"Seems kind of random."

"It's like a new group of settlers came to the prairie."

I thought about homesteading laws, and all the people who moved west thinking they were going to a farming paradise. Those people actually ended up in Oklahoma and northern Texas. "Were they tricked into thinking Minnesota was paradise?"

"Compared to war, it is paradise, don't you think?"

"Definitely. But there are forty-nine other states."

She shrugged. "For whatever reason, they moved to Minnesota. The Hmong mostly lived in Saint Paul, but the old people worried about the crime in the city and whether their kids would get in trouble, and they wanted to live in a small town where things are safe and clean and good for families. I heard that someone's kid was a fan of *Little House on the Prairie*, so she said, 'How about Walnut Grove?' And some of them moved here and sent word to their friends and families that it was a good place. More and more moved here, and now the town is twenty-five percent Hmong. Maybe even more. That's a bigger percentage of Asian people than in most big cities. So that's what I wrote about."

"Wow. I never thought about that. I've never lived in a small town so I didn't really notice. That's a really good essay. No wonder you won." My hot chocolate was cool enough to drink, so I gulped half of it.

"I thought Lanie would win."

"Who?"

"Lanie Erickson. She sits behind me. You know, Lanie."

"Curly Hair Girl?"

Julia raised her eyebrow. I covered my tracks. "Oh, *Lanie*. Right. Why'd you think she'd win?"

"She wrote that we should have a museum for Native Americans because they lived around here first, and they had these battles with settlers. She said the early farmers shouldn't be called settlers because the land was already settled. They were more like invaders." Julia leaned forward and whispered, "My grandma heard Mrs. Newman liked Lanie's essay because it showed critical thinking, but Gloria and Teresa said no way. Basically I was the second choice."

"Are you sure?"

"Grandma heard it from Connie Melby, who goes to church with Mrs. Newman's mother. I knew I'd won the essay contest two days before Mrs. Newman announced it."

By the time we left the diner, it was dark. Snow had melted during the day, and the puddles on the street were turning into mini ice-skating rinks. Even in thick-soled boots, you had to walk in slow, delicate steps with your legs wide apart. Rose and I called it the Minnesota duck walk.

"Let's cut through the park," I said.

Julia wrapped her scarf around her face. "Okay. It got cold fast."

Halfway to the picnic pavilion, I saw two people in the moonlight.

"Bad Chad," Julia whispered.

He spotted us before we could backtrack. I grabbed

Julia's coat sleeve and steered us to the left, but it was too late.

"It's the Little Museum on the Prairie girls!" Bad Chad shouted as he and his friend charged toward us. "Where's your covered wagon?" Even Bad Chad knew we worked at the museum, which was proof everyone knew everybody and everything in this town, including a guy so mean nobody talked to him.

The other guy said, "You going to the mercantile to buy a pencil and a slate?"

We ignored them and ran as fast as we could through the snow toward the street. A snowball hit my back. It felt like a rock. More snowballs zinged past but missed us. As soon as we got to the street, they stopped hollering. Julia looked back and said, "It's okay. They turned around."

"What a jerk," I said.

"I can think of better words than *jerk*," Julia said.

"Better not say them. It's Walnut Grove. Your grandma will hear about it before we get home."

You know what?

The sound of Julia's laughter was worth the pain from the snowball.

THIRTEEN

Christmas dinner was a flop. Rose wanted turkey, but turkeys are huge. Too big for four people, Mom said. She decided she'd get a chicken, but since a whole chicken is mostly bones, why not just get chicken meat? Boneless, skinless chicken breasts are expensive, though, so she bought frozen chicken strips and served them with creamed corn and runny instant mashed potatoes. She also planned to make a cake for dessert, but then she said she was too tired. We ended up smearing the canned frosting on crackers.

After dinner we opened presents. We got board games, hoodies, bags of caramel corn, and books. Rose hoisted her book in the air. "A Laura book! I can't wait to read it!"

"I thought you'd read them all," Freddy said.

"I have, but this isn't one of her novels. It's a biography of her life."

"Her novels are about her life," Freddy said. "Or am I missing something?"

"They're mostly about her life, but not entirely," Mom said. "She changed the timeline and left out lots of things that weren't appropriate for kids to read."

"Like what?" Rose asked.

Mom said, "Like witnessing alcoholism and violence and—"

"Prairie Madness," I said. "People went crazy because it was so hard to live here."

"Daddy is calling at five, so hurry and open my presents." Rose giggled as she handed each of us a small box. "You need to open them at the exact same time."

On the count of three, we ripped off the paper and opened the boxes. Rose beamed as we discovered we'd all received a mug, a stick of candy, and a shiny new penny.

"From *Little House on the Prairie*. Very clever!" Mom said.

I laughed so hard my eyes watered.

Rose said, "It's funny, but it's not that funny."

"Just wait." I handed out my gifts. "It will be."

When they opened my presents and discovered another mug, another candy stick, and another shiny new penny, they bent over laughing, too. If Freddy pulled the same gag gift, I thought, it'd be the perfect Christmas. He'd be the old Freddy with Twin Superpowers. Two birthdays in a row we'd given each other the same present—Harry

Potter posters the first time; supersized candy bars the second time.

But Freddy didn't give us boxes. He passed out three square flat packages. I knew what it was before I opened it: puppy calendars from the dollar store. I'd looked at them myself, but unlike Red Fred, I was sensitive to Rose's feelings and didn't want to make Rose think about Jack at Christmas.

Who was this weird boy and what had he done with my brother?

"Very sweet, Freddy." Mom hugged him.

Rose said, "Daddy is late."

Mom's body tensed up. "He probably doesn't have good cell phone reception."

"You should call him," Freddy suggested. "He's in a different time zone. I bet he got the schedule messed up."

Rose shrugged. "It's okay. He's probably too busy meeting my new family and telling them about me."

"Of course," Mom said. "There are so many wonderful things to tell."

Rose wiped her eyes. "I have to go to the bathroom. I'll be out in a minute."

Mom's jaw clenched as Rose slammed the bathroom door. "I'd strangle him if I could."

I nearly gasped. Mom didn't talk like that. Negative words breed negative thinking, and negative thinking creates an atmosphere of sadness and despair. That's what she always said.

"I'd strangle him, too," Freddy said. "Then I'd spit on him."

"Freddy!" I waited for Mom to turn the rain into a rainbow, but she crossed her arms and sighed.

A few minutes later Rose came back with a smile on her face. "I have the best idea ever. Mom, get your guitar. We can go Christmas caroling."

It was the worst idea ever. It would be like when we were little and Mom would drag us to the beach to sing for the tourists, and they'd toss dollar bills into her guitar case. It'd be like that only seventy degrees colder.

"It's too cold," I said.

"Yeah, the cold might damage my hearing aids." I knew Freddy wouldn't go along with it. He was Red Fred, but he wasn't crazy.

"Leave them here," Rose said. "We'll be loud because we're singing. You'll hear just fine."

"Won't the cold make your fingers too stiff to play guitar?" Freddy asked.

"I'm willing to try." Mom patted Rose's back. "I think we could all use a mood-lifting activity. Let's do it."

Fifteen minutes later we were singing "Jingle Bells" in front of a white house across the street. The old man and woman at the door were Hmong, and I couldn't tell if they understood English. I couldn't tell if they celebrated Christmas. What I could tell was they were shivering.

When we paused after the first verse, the woman clapped her hands. The man said, "Very nice," and shut the door.

Mom blew into her hands. "I don't think I can play. My fingers are stiff."

"Told you," Freddy said.

"We'll just sing," Rose said. "We don't need the guitar."

"Good idea." Mom pulled on her gloves as we did the Minnesota duck walk to the next house. Rose rang the bell, and we launched into "Deck the Halls" as soon as the door opened. The woman smiled and wrapped her arms around herself as we fa-la-la-la-la'd. My teeth chattered through the next verse, and Freddy dropped out entirely because he started coughing. When we hit the last note, a man stuck his head out the door.

"The famous author sings!" It was Shorty from the gas station. Mom shifted awkwardly, but she smiled.

The lady said, "I'm Shorty's sister, Joan. You must be freezing. Come inside and warm up."

Before we could politely decline—it was their Christmas, after all—Rose hopped through the door.

"Rose!" Mom said. "We need to—"

"You need to come inside and have some pie. That's what you need to do," Shorty said. "Come on in."

Between Mom and Rose and their stranger-loving ways, we'd probably be there until midnight, and we'd probably leave with invitations to New Year's dinner. And a batch of gizzard soup.

But that's not what happened.

You know what Mom said?

She said, "No."

Our mom, Rainbow Queen Martha Lake, said no.

Our Twin Superpowers sparked for a moment. Freddy

141

stared at me like, *What's going on?* I stared back at him like, *I can't believe it!* Then the connection fizzled. The phone in his pocket must have vibrated with a text, because he pulled it out and read it. Red Fred was so popular kids were texting him on Christmas.

Rose peered through the door. She already had her coat off. "The pie smells amazing. They have cookies, too."

"Rose, they're having a family meal," Mom said. "Let's go."

Shorty said, "We ate hours ago. Everyone pretty much left. Come inside or you'll offend my sister, and everyone in town will hear about it."

I couldn't tell if Mom was blushing or if her cheeks were red from the cold. Rose said, "It's a Christmas adventure, right?" We all shivered and waited for Mom to answer. Mom finally nodded, and we went inside.

Joan introduced us to her husband, Harry, and Harry's cousin Eric and Eric's wife, Stacy.

Eric said, "Cold enough for ya?"

We nodded.

"The kids have gone home," Joan said. "Have a seat, and I'll get the pie. We finished the cherry pie, but I have two whole apple pies left."

"We love apple pie," I said.

"Our dessert was crackers with frosting." Rose wrinkled her nose.

Joan laughed. "Well, that's different."

Mom looked embarrassed. If Joan believed Rose's story, in two days everyone in town would be talking about the weird writer lady and her frosting-and-crackers dessert. So I said, "Rose is hilarious!" Rose pressed her lips together and didn't correct me. She got the hint.

Shorty sat next to Mom. "You write books *and* play guitar *and* sing?"

"Mom plays piano, too." Rose helped herself to a cookie from a tray on the coffee table. She licked frosting off her finger. I couldn't help myself. I took a cookie, too—a cookie shaped like a Christmas tree with green icing. Delicious. "Can she play your piano?" Rose asked. "We could sing carols right here."

Sure enough, in the corner of the room was an upright piano.

Shorty said, "Yes," just as Mom said, "No."

"That'd be nice." Joan handed out plates of apple pie, which had scoops of ice cream and drizzles of caramel. I put the cookie down so I could eat the pie right away, because it was warm. It was so good I wanted to swallow it whole. "My daughter played piano, but she went off to college, and now it just sits here all lonely and out of tune."

"We'll just eat your wonderful pie and go. I'm sorry to impose."

"Not at all," Joan said.

"Not at all," Harry said.

"Not one little bit," Shorty said.

Eric's and Stacy's mouths were full of pie, so they just nodded.

"We didn't get to church today, which is terrible, I

know," Joan said. "I had my hands full with getting dinner ready. I think 'Silent Night' would be good for the soul. My daughter has a whole book of Christmas music."

"I suppose I could play 'Silent Night.'" Mom sat at the piano and tinkered with the keys to jog her memory while Joan looked for the music. I prepared myself for embarrassment. With Mom, one song always turned into ten. I hoped she didn't put her hat on the floor to collect donations. I looked at Freddy and tried to spark our Superpowers, but he was checking the phone.

So I thought really hard and tried to find a rainbow instead of focusing on the potential embarrassment. If Mom kept singing, maybe Joan would offer me another piece of pie. She might even send us home with a bag of her cookies. That was the kind of neighborly thing people in Walnut Grove did. Gizzard soup. Pie. Cookies.

Rose scooted next to me. "See! A sisters' Christmas adventure!"

"Sure," I said through a mouthful of pie.

Mom started "Silent Night," and Joan stood next to the piano. I knew Mom's voice was pretty, but it sounded different with Joan's. Their voices were magical together, sweet and joyful and moving. Shorty's forkful of pie was frozen in midair, like he was too impressed to put it in his mouth. Harry closed his eyes. I swear Eric wiped a tear from his cheek.

When they finished, everyone clapped and whooped.

You know who asked for another song?

Me.

· **CHAPTER** ·

FOURTEEN

Miguel brought a box of winter gear downstairs and put it on the kitchen table. Ethan had invited Freddy to spend the rest of Christmas break on an ice-fishing trip in northern Minnesota. Regular winter clothes wouldn't cut it.

"Most of these are things my grandsons used to wear," Miguel said.

Freddy pulled out a pair of sunglasses. "I don't think I'll need these."

"Sunglasses are important," Miguel said. "The lake is covered with snow, and when the sun's rays hit the snow, it's like staring into the sun. Your eyes can be damaged. It's called snow blindness." He handed Freddy a pair of boots. "These boots are rated for temperatures of forty below, but they might be too small."

"They look close enough," Rose said.

Miguel shook his head. "If they're even a little bit tight, your circulation gets cut off, and your feet will freeze. Never wear tight boots. Very dangerous."

Mom held up two spikes connected by a wire. "And what's this contraption?"

"Ice picks," Miguel said. "If the ice breaks and you fall in, it's impossible to crawl out because the ice is slippery and there's nothing to hold on to. You need to stab the ice with a pick and use it to pull yourself out."

Mom swallowed hard. "I'm not sure I like this."

"I'll be fine, Mom," Freddy said.

"What about a life jacket?" Mom asked.

"If he falls in, he won't drown," Miguel said. "He'll die from hypothermia first."

I waited for Mom to change her mind, to say Freddy should definitely open himself to possibilities—just not *this* possibility. She sighed. Rose sighed.

"Maybe I'll come home with fish to eat. It's going to be fun, Mom."

"Or Mom could buy fish sticks," I said. "Then only the fish are dead."

Freddy didn't laugh. He rolled his eyes. Miguel said, "Ethan's dad knows what he's doing. Once they get settled in the ice house, they'll be comfortable. They'll watch TV and eat leftover pie."

"TV?" I couldn't believe it. "How do they get electricity?"

"Generators. Those ice houses are little castles. They've got TVs, DVD players, music, microwaves. Everything you can imagine." Miguel dug into the box and pulled out skates. "And these are for you, Charlotte. Julia wants to take you ice-skating."

Freddy smirked. "She won't go."

"Well, we're leaving in an hour." Miguel put the skates in front of me. "Would you like to go?"

I could barely walk in boots, and Julia wanted me to glide on ice basically wearing shoes with razor blades?

Hah!

You know what I said?

I smirked right back at Red Fred. "No, I wouldn't *like* to go. I'd *love* to go."

I'm full of surprises, right?

. . . . .

I fell ten times in ten minutes. Each time Julia pulled me up and held my arms until I was steady. A dozen kids had converged on a pond outside of town. I recognized some of them from school. Two kindergartners had hockey sticks but no puck. One girl didn't have skates. She glided around the pond on her boots.

"I should do that." I pointed to the girl. "Boot skating."

"You can do it. Relax. Go with the flow," Julia said. "You're jerking around because you're scared of falling.

Don't think about walking. Put your foot forward and then push to the side and back, like you're trying to push something off the sidewalk. *Flow*."

"Okay. No walking. Just flowing."

I imagined there was a crumbled-up ball of paper in front of me, and I needed to push it to the side with my foot. The mental picture helped—I wobbled to the other side of the pond without falling.

Julia cheered.

"Are my legs supposed to feel like noodles?"

"Once you get the hang of it, you'll be fine."

She effortlessly circled around me. I stumbled as I turned and used the forward-push technique to cross the pond again. I did it over and over, a little faster each time. My cheeks ached from the cold, yet I was sweating. My hair felt wet under my hat, and I could feel sweat trickle down my back. Sweating in the winter!

How was that even possible?

"You're a natural," Julia said. "I bet you could learn to skate backward. You could probably do a spin."

I laughed. "Next time, okay?"

Flowing was a good word. That's how skating felt once I got the hang of it. Not *floating*, because I felt attached to the ground, but *flowing*. I lost track of time. I even forgot about being cold. I went around and around the pond without a stumble until Julia grabbed my arm.

"Getting hungry?"

I had to think about it. "I guess."

"Let's get something to eat." As we skated toward our stuff, Julia said, "Let's have a skating party with Bao and Emma sometime. We can have a sleepover, too. Want to?"

I bit my lip and shrugged. "Maybe."

"Jeez, Charlotte! What girl says maybe to a party?"

I was the girl who said *no* to parties, right? But I thought about Truth or Dare and the lunchroom conversations and working with Julia in the museum. Then I thought about that moment—Julia cheering for me while I wobbled across the pond. It was nice to have someone cheer for me, someone who didn't have to cheer just because I was a daughter or a sister. Actually, the people who'd been my cheerleaders lately weren't my family. Mrs. Newman. Gloria. Teresa. Julia. I thought about a sleepover with Julia, Bao, and Emma. Even though I tried to have no reaction, I felt a smile spread across my face.

Was I the kind of girl who said yes to parties?

Maybe. Maybe I was that kind of girl.

"There's Grandpa." Julia pointed to the road. "Grandma said we can have cookies and hot chocolate when we get home."

"Good timing. I'm hungry and freezing."

Back at the house, Mia let us bring a plate of cookies and our drinks into Julia's bedroom. We sat on beanbag chairs and listened to a playlist Julia had made. She was quiet, and I realized she'd been cheering for me all morning, so it was probably my turn to ask her a question.

"How was your Christmas and the dad visit?"

Julia made a face. "He gave me a doll. I haven't played with dolls in two years. He doesn't even know me. Then he argued with my grandpa."

"It was a bad-dad day in our house, too," I said. "Rose's dad forgot to call her."

"That's awful. What about your dad? Is he dead or something? I mean, if you don't want to talk about it, that's okay."

"My parents broke up when we were little, and my mom thought he was a bad guy, so we don't see him."

"I'm sorry. That stinks."

I shrugged. "Rose used to visit her dad, but now he's totally focused on his new wife. Rose feels terrible. I think it's better to not have a dad than to have one and watch him turn into a jerk. I just assume my dad is a jerk. Then I don't miss him."

Julia thought about what I said. "He probably has some good points. All people have something good inside them."

"I think people show their bad sides most of the time. If you're a good person, you have to be careful or you'll get crushed."

"You really think so?"

"Of course. There are more mean people than good people."

"When my dad robbed Shorty's gas station, some of the

150

kids were really mean to me. Jake Carson called me a jail-bird."

"See?"

"But there were also kids who didn't say anything at all. They stayed out of it. And there were kids like Emma and Bao. They sat with me at lunch and hung out with me at recess. They invited me to their birthday parties."

"Just Emma and Bao? You made my point."

"They were enough. Before the robbery, I thought it would be great to be popular like Katie Turner and have everyone want to be my friend. But afterward, I realized I'd rather have two amazing friends than a bunch of people who just follow me around because I have expensive clothes and cute hair and the fanciest house in town."

Julia had gambled on Emma and Bao, and she got lucky. It could've gone the other way. In Atlanta, there were two kids at school who pretended we had a lot in common because they were twins, too. But I could tell they were faking it, and sure enough, after a week they stopped talking to us.

"And now we're all friends," Julia said. "You and me and Emma and Bao."

I realized I felt warm inside, and it wasn't from the hot chocolate. It was Julia—Julia and Emma and Bao. I could have three friends. They were right there, right in front of me with parties and sleepovers. We'd move at some point, but Mom obviously needed more time to finish the book. A lot more time. If she kept a pace of five words over five months, we'd never leave Laura and the prairie.

Friends.

Julia said, "That's pretty cool, right?"

Finally I said, "Yes. It's cool."

You know what?

I even meant it.

· **CHAPTER** ·

FIFTEEN

We didn't go back to school at the end of break. The radio reported school was canceled because of cold weather. Minnesota was so cold we got two temperature reports— one being the regular temperature and the other being the regular temperature plus wind. In the winter, the regular temperature could kill you. The regular temperature plus a wind chill could kill you faster. That day the temperature was minus fifteen, and the wind chill was minus forty.

"It's literally colder than the inside of our freezer." Mom wrapped herself in a blanket and shivered. "A polar bear would die in this weather."

I decided to point out a rainbow. "At least we're not sweating. Remember Atlanta in July?"

Mom snorted. "I fantasize about Atlanta in July."

My mother didn't snort.

Who was this person?

I tried another approach. "We get to have a family day! We can play games."

"You could read the beginning of the Mars book to us," Rose said. "I really want to hear it."

"Good idea," Freddy said.

Mom peeled off the blanket and opened the refrigerator. "I should've picked up groceries yesterday. There's nothing in the house."

"What about the leftover pizza?" Freddy asked.

"I checked," Rose said. "It's moldy. We have tuna and popcorn."

Mom got her coat from the closet. She wrapped a scarf around her face, pulled a hat down to her eyebrows, and stuffed her hands in mittens. "I'll go to the Asian grocery and get stuff for stir-fry. Anyone want to come?"

Freddy and Rose took a pass, but I thought it'd be good for Mom to have company. When Mom and I stepped onto the driveway, I inhaled and got an instant case of brain freeze, like I'd stuffed ice cubes in my nose. Every breath felt like a knife stabbing my head and then my chest. Even my eyeballs hurt.

We hustled to the car. My pants were no protection from the cold. The car's seat felt like a block of ice, and our breath looked like plumes of smoke when we exhaled. Mom turned the key, but the engine protested. *Rrrurrrurr.* She tried again. *Rrrurrrurr.* On the third try, the engine didn't even moan. There was nothing but a faint click. Mom banged her head against the steering wheel. "Is this really happening?"

"Maybe we can borrow Miguel's car."

She sighed. "Mia texted me. They went to visit family last night and decided to stay because of the weather."

"Let's go back inside."

"Wait." She put her hand on my leg. "Let's put some positive energy out there. We get what we give. That's what I believe, right? If we put our desire into the universe, the universe answers."

Now Mom chose to think about positive energy? "My face hurts."

"Charlotte, please. I'm desperate. Energy."

I closed my eyes and tried to be quiet, but I couldn't stop my teeth from chattering. I thought good thoughts. I imagined the sound of the car starting. I imagined the heater blasting warm air. I imagined the taste of warm rice and soy sauce.

"Okay," Mom said. "I'm going to turn the key, and the car is going to start."

She turned the key. Nothing. Just the click of a dead engine.

She said it louder. "The car is going to start."

Nothing.

"Say it, Charlotte."

Through chattering teeth I said, "The c-c-c-car will st-st-start."

Nothing.

"The car will start! This car will start right now or I swear to God I'll—" Mom hit the steering wheel, and the horn gave a feeble honk.

"Mom!" I grabbed her arm. "Stop!"

This wasn't my mom. My mom didn't sigh or snort or hit. Mom took a few deep breaths and said, "Forget it. Let's go inside."

Mom marched downstairs and went into the bathroom without a word. I sat on the sofa next to Rose. "The car won't start. It's like the battery is frozen—literally frozen. Where's Freddy?"

"He's in his room with the phone."

"Of course." I snorted, which was normal. I was supposed to be the snorter in the family, not Mom.

Rose took Mom's phone from her purse. "I have an idea." She went into our room and shut the door as Mom barreled out of the bathroom with a hair dryer. She had a wild look in her eye. She hoisted it over her head and shouted, "The universe will respond!"

She marched upstairs. Freddy poked his head from his room. "What's going on?"

"Observation: Mom is losing it," I said as I ran to catch up to her.

Mom dug through a shelf in the garage until she found an extension cord. She plugged the hair dryer into the extension cord and the extension cord into an outlet.

"What are you doing?" Freddy's coat was unzipped,

156

and he didn't have a hat or mittens. He stayed close to the basement door for warmth.

Mom didn't answer him. She pressed the button on the wall. A blast of cold hit us as the garage door opened. The end of her scarf rippled like a flag as she walked into the wind. We stood in the garage and shivered while she opened the hood of the car, turned on the hair dryer, and placed it on the engine. She carefully pulled down the hood but didn't latch it.

"Now what?" Freddy asked me.

"I have no idea."

Mom adjusted her scarf and came back to the garage. "I'll give it fifteen minutes."

I cleared my throat. "Mom, I'm pretty sure you can't start a car with a hair dryer."

"Pretty sure," Freddy agreed.

"It's a test for the universe. If the car starts, we stay in one place until I finish the book. If it doesn't start, we bounce around until something sticks—"

Freddy's face went pale. "That's insane!"

"Something has to change," Mom said.

I didn't know if my heart was pounding from excitement or anger. I only knew it was beating against my ribs. Moving? We'd escape the empty prairie, the basement, the winter. That was good.

Right?

But it didn't feel good at all. It felt bad. I didn't know what to say.

Freddy knew. "I'm not moving. I don't care what the universe says. I don't care what you say."

Mom said, "Freddy, we're a family. We stick together."

"You are the one with the hearing problem," he said. "I said I'm not leaving. I'll live with Mia and Miguel. I'll get a job and pay rent."

"That's ridiculous."

"Even Charlotte likes it here, and she hates everything."

The words *I do not!* were lodged in my throat, but I couldn't get them out. I couldn't believe he'd said that about me. I felt frozen inside. Freddy looked away and squinted. "Who's that?"

A truck had pulled up next to our car. A man in a snowsuit and a ski mask stepped out. He followed the extension cord into the garage and pulled off his mask. It was Shorty from the gas station.

"Hi, Martha."

Mom blinked in surprise. "What are you doing here?"

"Your little girl called the station and said your car won't start. Happens all the time if you keep it outside."

"As you can see, it's under control. But thank you."

"I brought jumper cables. It won't take long."

"You're very kind," Mom loosened her scarf. "But I'm used to dealing with problems myself. In fact, I'm warming up the battery right now."

"With a hair dryer." I said it without sarcasm or anger because inside I was too empty and cold for emotion.

Freddy had said I hate everything—Freddy, who used to agree with me 100 percent.

"We're testing the universe. If the car starts, we'll stay. If it won't, we're moving. Because that's how reasonable people make decisions." Freddy hadn't lost his sarcasm.

Shorty didn't know what to say. He raised an eyebrow and nodded. Finally he said, "I guess it's no different than flipping a quarter. People do that all the time."

"Thank you," Mom said.

"You bet," Shorty said.

We huddled in the back of the garage, out of the wind, but nobody spoke. Finally Shorty leaned against Miguel's toolbox and said, "Winter's hard, even for me, and I grew up here."

Mom smiled. "The snow is beautiful."

"Yup," Shorty said. "But it's hard."

"I love the way the frost covers the trees."

"Yup. But it's hard."

"The sun—"

"Just say it's hard!" Freddy said through clenched teeth.

Mom sighed. "It's hard, okay? Happy now?" She sighed again. "It's time to find out what the universe has to say."

As Mom trudged down the driveway, Freddy turned to me. "What kind of vibes are you putting into the universe right now? Leaving vibes? Or staying vibes?"

"I hate everything, remember?"

"Jeez, I didn't mean it."

"Hah!"

He leaned against the garage wall, crossed his arms, and stared at the car, like he was willing it to start.

I thought about his question. I was making something here. Maybe my online scrapbook wasn't as brilliant as Gloria thought, but it was good. Really good. I was sharing the story of Laura and Walnut Grove with the world. I wasn't doing it for money, and I wasn't doing it as a punishment, either, because I never cheated on my essay. I was doing it because I wanted to make something.

And I had three friends, three real-deal friends. Emma, Bao, and Julia.

Rainbow-denier Charlotte Lake had three friends.

We had to stay.

Please.

Mom turned off the hair dryer and got into the car. I sent a message to the universe: *Start our stupid car NOW.*

Rrrurrrurr.

"Don't pump the gas. You'll flood it," Shorty said under his breath.

Rrrurrrurr.

"Don't pump the gas!" Freddy shouted. "You'll flood it!"

Rrrurrrurr.

I held my breath and Freddy yelled, "C'mon!"

Rrrurrrurr.

Vroooom!

The engine caught and roared to life.

Shorty shook his head. "Well, now I've seen everything."

Freddy pumped his fist in the air and shrieked. He tried

to high-five me, but I just shrugged and said, "Sorry. Too busy hating everything."

While the car warmed up, Mom walked back to the garage.

Shorty said, "I guess my services aren't needed. I better get back to the station."

"You are very sweet to come over. I'm sorry Rose bothered you." Mom's eyes sparkled with her victory.

"Not a bother," he said. "Get yourself an engine block warmer. I'll install it, and you can keep the hair dryer in the bathroom."

You know what Mom did?

She didn't snort or sigh.

She hugged him.

. . . . .

I couldn't sleep that night.

Yes, the car had started, and that was good.

But Freddy's words played over and over in my mind. *She hates everything.* I tried to replace his words with song lyrics. Lady Gaga. The Beatles. Beyoncé. When that didn't work, I silently recited the Pledge of Allegiance a couple of times. Still his words wouldn't leave. I even got a flashlight and read a chapter from *The First Transcontinental Railroad: The Impact of Westward Expansion on American Culture and the Economy.*

Finally I shook Rose's shoulder.

"What's wrong?" she mumbled.

"Do I hate everything?"

"Huh?"

"Move over." I squeezed next to her. "Do I hate everything? I need to know."

She yawned. "Not everything. Just most things."

"You're wrong." I turned to the side and leaned on my elbow. "I'm not a negative person. I'll name things I like. The list is long, because I'm so positive. I like *The Hunger Games* series and—"

"Can I point out that *The Hunger Games* is about kids who are forced to kill one another?"

"No. You cannot. I also like happy movies like *Toy Story*. I like chocolate chip cookies and swimming and Monopoly and dogs and carrots and . . . What kid likes carrots? Me. I like so many things I even like carrots."

"Why are we doing this?"

I pulled the blanket to my chin and sighed. "Freddy said I hate everything."

"Freddy is stupid." Mom taught us *stupid* was a swear word. Rose didn't sigh or snort or hit, and she never, ever said *stupid*. "He thinks Mom can be talked into staying here," she continued, "and that's not going to happen."

"Mom got a signal from the universe. She's going to finish the book here in Walnut Grove, and trust me, that's going to take a long, long time."

Rose sat up. "How do you know?"

"I snooped. I opened her laptop when she was asleep.

She's only written five words. That's why I know we'll be here a long time, and I think it's good. See how positive I am?"

"She's doing research. Research takes time."

Rose could find reasons for anything. Mom wasn't failing at writing. She was succeeding at research! All this made me think about the frozen battery and Shorty's visit. "Rose, why did you call Shorty?"

"To help Mom with the car," she said innocently.

"Why'd you *really* call Shorty?"

She sighed in surrender. "Fine. I want to stay here, too. And he obviously has a crush on Mom, so maybe she'll get a crush on him if she gives him a chance. So I called."

I rubbed my chin. "Wait a minute! Did you know his sister Joan lived in that house when we went Christmas caroling? And that he'd be there?"

"Maybe Mia is friends with Joan's neighbor. Maybe Mia told me."

"Maybe?"

Rose shrugged. "Maybe Mia knows Shorty is single and that Joan always hosts their family's Christmas."

I laughed. I couldn't help it.

"So you want to stay in Walnut Grove? What about adventure?"

"It's small and safe and not expensive. And this is the first place where you and I really hang out. Freddy has his own thing. But here you and I can be a team."

"Yeah," I said. Wow. Rose truly was the world's best rainbow-finder if I was her substitute for actual friends.

Rose sighed.

"What?"

"The other day Mom talked about Houston. She said being close to the space station might help her connect with the Mars story."

"But today she said if the car started, we'd stay here until she finished . . ." My voice trailed off. "Wait a minute. She didn't say we'd stay *here* until she finished the book. She said we'd stay in one place."

"I wonder if that place is Houston."

"But she didn't say anything about Houston. Let me think. She said if the car started, we'd stay in one place. If it didn't start, we'd bounce around until something stuck."

"So she didn't say Walnut Grove specifically?"

My heart pounded all over again. "No."

"Should we ask her?"

"Absolutely not! She'll think the universe planted the Houston idea in your head. She'll think it's meant to be or something crazy like that."

"So we're just supposed to wonder?"

"Let me think about it, okay?"

Rose yawned. "Okay."

If Rose had told me about Houston a few weeks ago, it would've been fine. Just another move. Why in the world did I stop my lunchtime reading with Mrs. Newman and start hanging out with those kids? How could I have been so stupid? For a moment, I tried to convince myself Rose had it all wrong. But Rose understood Mom better than any of us. When it came to Mom, Rose was right. She was always right.

Gets old, doesn't it?

SIXTEEN

We were home for three days before the guy on the radio announced a warming trend. He said temperatures would rise to four degrees above zero, and the schools would open Thursday.

Julia, Freddy, Rose, and I left the house at the same time and trudged through the snow. We couldn't talk because we'd wrapped scarves around our faces, leaving a small opening for our eyes. Bao waved at me when we walked through the school door. I pretended not to see her. Emma said, "Hey there!" as she passed my locker, but I pretended I didn't hear. When the bell rang at lunchtime, I got my backpack from my locker and spread my lunch on my desk.

Mrs. Newman crossed her arms. "Charlotte? What are you doing?"

I just wanted to hide in the classroom like before. If we moved to Houston, my new friends would be strangers again, but I couldn't tell Mrs. Newman that. She'd give me one of those "all's well that ends well" lectures, like Ma Ingalls always gave. She'd say we'd stay in touch and be lifelong friends, all thanks to the Internet. I was almost old enough to have online accounts, but it wouldn't matter. Not really. Even if the girls talked to me online, what would we talk about? We wouldn't be part of each other's stories. It's not like we could have online ice-skating parties.

"You wanted me to read that Trail of Tears article, and I haven't. I figured you have another copy, and I could do it now."

"You had the entire Christmas break plus three school-cancellation days to read it. You're telling me you haven't even started it?"

"I knew you'd be mad, so that's why I brought my lunch. I knew you'd want me to read it now."

Mrs. Newman crossed her arms. She did not fake smile. "Take your lunch to the cafeteria and eat with the kids. If there's a problem, hiding in the classroom can't be your first choice. Try to resolve it. I'll expect you to finish that article over the weekend."

She shuffled the papers on her desk, which told me the discussion was closed.

At lunch, the girls around me talked about their Christmas presents. New phones. New tablets. Gift cards. Bao told us about her aunt's terrible cooking. Julia told us Miguel slipped on the ice and hurt his back. Emma told us her brother left a can of Coke in the car, and it froze and exploded.

I wanted to tell them about our frosted-cracker dessert, Christmas Day caroling, and Mom starting the car with a hair dryer. But I stayed quiet. I stared at my lunch and ate the corn one kernel at a time.

After school I told Julia I had a headache. She went to the museum alone, and I went home and headed straight to my bedroom. Rose was lying on her bed with the Laura biography she got for Christmas. She handed our phone to me.

"You have a text message."

The message was from Julia. *Gloria brought cookies. I'll bring some home for you. Feel better soon!*

Rose put the book in the drawer of the nightstand. "I'm not going to finish this biography. Don't tell Mom. I don't want to hurt her feelings. Do you want to read it?"

"Why wouldn't you finish it?"

"It's not like Laura's books. It's boring and sad."

"But it's Laura. You love Laura." I searched through the stack of books and papers on the floor. "Hey, have you seen an article with Trail of Tears in the title? I have to read it, or Mrs. Newman's laser eyes might blast me into oblivion."

"I think it's in that stack of newspapers on the table. I read it."

"You must be bored if you're reading my schoolwork." I sat down next to her. "Why don't you ever hang out with friends anymore?"

She shrugged. "It's cold outside."

"You don't have to be outside."

"I know."

"What's wrong?"

"Nothing!" Rose nearly shouted at me.

"Jeez."

It didn't sound like nothing, so I took the phone to the kitchen table and checked her texts. I saw a message from her dad. He'd said, *I'm working on a new ship now, so I might not get time off during your spring break. I hope we can have the whole month of July together.* She'd replied, *YAY! A new ship! How fun! And cool! Love you!*

Five exclamation points?

Even for Rose, that was a record.

· · · · ·

A few days later, temperatures warmed enough for icicles to start melting. During the day, you could hear them *drip drip drip.* I thought this was a good sign, but Mrs. Newman warned us not to stand under them, because if the heavy ones broke, we'd end up with a concussion or worse.

Prairie winters were so dangerous you could die from icicle injuries.

Mom and I were at Shorty's gas station buying milk when we saw Mia.

"Cold enough for ya?" she asked.

"At least the melting means spring is coming," Mom said.

"Spring? Oh, Martha!" Mia laughed like a crazy comic book villain. "This is the January thaw. It happens every year. Mother Nature teases us with a few warm days, and then KABOOM!" She got right in my face when she *kaboomed*. I nearly jumped out of my snow boots. She laughed again. "You guys are definitely from Florida."

"I was born in Delaware," I said. "We lived in Florida. And North Carolina and Kentucky and Illinois. But Illinois was in the summer."

"You don't have a strong southern accent at all. Just a hint. I'm losing my accent. My parents moved from Mexico to Texas when I was little."

"We watch a lot of TV. Pretty much everyone sounds the same on TV."

"You know what's funny?" Mia leaned close and quietly said, "Minnesotans think everybody else has an accent. They don't even notice how they say *Minnahsooooootah*."

Mia laughed, and I tried to laugh, too, but it wasn't easy. I kept thinking about how much I'd miss her. I still hadn't asked Mom about Houston. It was too risky. Mom would take a question about Houston from one of her kids as a sign we were meant to go there. Rose said it was probably smart to assume we were going, that we should make a pledge to stay best-sister-friends forever and turn the move into an adventure.

Mia asked, "Now where'd your mother wander off to?"

Sure enough, Mom was gone. I looked around the shelf, and she was at the register talking to Shorty and laughing.

Mia whispered, "Shorty got divorced last year. Let's just say his wife was in love with something else. The credit card!"

"Really?"

"Keep that information to yourself."

"I will."

As I watched them talk, I wondered if Rose's plan could actually work. Even if it did, was it a good idea? Mom didn't have luck with men. My dad broke her heart. Rey broke her heart. Other boyfriends broke her heart.

I felt all mixed up inside.

"He's a handsome man, isn't he?" Mia winked at me.

Under my breath I said, "He probably isn't the man you think he is."

"What?"

I nodded. "Yes, Mia. He's very handsome."

. . . . .

As everyone headed to gym the next day, Mrs. Newman told me to stay in the classroom. Finally. She'd given me a bunch of extensions for reading the article. My reasons for not finishing it: I had to take care of my little sister because Mom had a headache, I had to help shovel the driveway because Miguel hurt his back, an icicle broke and hit me on the head, I couldn't find the article, Mom thought it was an old note so she threw it away.

A pretty good list, don't you think? I was running out of excuses. Eventually she'd have to make me stay in the classroom at lunch.

She crossed her arms and stared with her bullet eyes. There was no fake smile. "Charlotte, I see your little plan to get out of the cafeteria, and it's not going to work. I left a voice mail message for your mother. I'm going to discuss this with her."

This didn't worry me too much. Mom would probably tell Mrs. Newman that children need the freedom to explore their lunch options. "I can read the article after school today. My sister read it first and somehow it ended up under her bed. That's one hundred percent true."

"Would you like to tell me what's going on? Your work was extraordinary before break."

I shook my head. "Nothing is going on."

"I asked the lunch supervisor if you're having trouble with the kids, and she said everything seems fine. Is it?"

"Yes." And it was fine. I had a place to sit. Nobody tried

to bully me. All I had to do was stay out of the conversation. Not laugh, not talk. And whenever someone said, "Is something wrong?" I just had to say, "I have a headache again." I reminded myself every single day that I would never see these people again.

Mrs. Newman said, "I'm going to talk to your mother about sending you to school early so you can catch up."

"But I need my sleep."

"Then it sounds like you have a choice: get your work done and sleep longer, or get up early, come to school, and finish assignments in the classroom."

I felt my face burn red from frustration. "Look, we're moving. Maybe to Houston next week. Maybe somewhere else next month. That's what we do—we move! I won't be here, so it doesn't matter."

I rushed out of the classroom before she could pretend to feel sorry for me.

. . . . .

After school, I didn't wait for Julia. I walked to the museum by myself and got the digital camera. When we photographed the artifacts in the cases, like the old school slates and dainty handkerchiefs, Gloria used special gloves to remove them. She set the items on a table, and one of us took a picture, and the other wrote a description on a pad of paper. Later we uploaded the photos into the computer and typed up the descriptions.

I could get started without Julia. I hung up my coat in the break room and walked to the storage room to let Gloria know I'd arrived. She was talking to Teresa, and I heard worried voices say something about "budget" and "money." I stopped outside the door and listened.

"What are we going to do?" Teresa asked.

Gloria said, "I don't think we can pay for the work. How'd an accounting mistake like this happen? It's terrible."

"It's no use crying over spilled milk. Maybe we can ask for the work to be a donation."

Julia wasn't going to get paid?

Gloria let out a long, frustrated sigh. "It should be a donation. Frankly, the quality isn't there. I don't make a fuss, because I don't like fusses, but I'm not impressed by their work in the least."

My online scrapbook!

I felt my stomach clench. They didn't think it was brilliant. They lied. All my ideas, all those photos, the sorting, the writing, the uploading, the designing . . . I had to press my lips together to keep from yelling. Gloria and Teresa were worse than fake-nice. They were mean and cruel, a team of senior citizen Nellie Olesons.

Laura's spirit would be angrier than a prairie blizzard.

Teresa sighed and said, "Let's keep this information to ourselves for the time being. We can think it over. We're gonna have company in a few minutes, if you know what I mean."

SEVENTEEN

I marched on the icy sidewalk toward home. No careful Minnesota duck walk for me.

Right! Left! Right! Left!

Stomp! Stomp! Stomp! Stomp!

I'd been in the break room when Julia had called hello from the front of the museum. I was sitting at the table, pretending like I'd been waiting there the whole time. Gloria and Teresa entered with fake smiles on their faces, joking about being forgetful because of frozen brains. But I was so mad I couldn't pretend I heard something funny. My face must have looked sour, because Gloria patted my shoulder and said, "No pouting, kiddo. Let's get to work."

I'd said something about having a terrible headache and rushed outside without another word.

Now I was outside, but the frigid temperatures didn't cool my anger. How dare they trash-talk my idea? And even consider not paying Julia?

I arrived home and stomped down the stairs with the full weight of my boots. I was going to tell Mom exactly what had happened. She'd be shocked at the negative thoughts this town put into the universe.

But when I burst into the living room, she looked up from her laptop, and her eyes were as cold as Mrs. Newman's. She pointed to the couch. "Take off your boots and have a seat."

I took my time getting out of my boots. I wasn't eager to find out what it meant when Mom's eyes looked cold. Finally I sat down.

"What is going on, Charlotte? You're missing assignments. Your work is below average. I don't understand—"

"Mrs. Newman is out to get me. I'll do better in the next school. I promise."

"Is that what you told her? You'll do better in the next school? Because what she told me is my children might benefit by staying in the same location." She stood and paced the floor. "So thanks for leaving her with the impression that I'm not stable."

"I didn't say anything bad."

"You said enough."

I blinked back tears. "I just said we're moving. That's all. Are we going . . . somewhere like . . . another city, maybe in the south that has something to do with the space program?"

Mom blinked a few times. "It's a strong possibility."

"It's also a strong possibility that moving us right now will make us unstable!"

Mom shouted, "I'm doing the best I can!"

"So am I!" I yelled.

Rose stepped out of the bedroom. "What's going on?"

"Mrs. Newman is causing problems, and Mom's blaming me." Mom started to respond, but I cut her off. "It's not my fault!"

As Mom paced the floor, I noticed something: she wasn't waddling around in pajamas. Her hair was tucked in a bun, and she wore black jeans, a dark red sweater, and lipstick.

Something was different.

Even though it looked like something was *better*, it felt wrong.

"Charlotte, I'm very—"

"Why are you dressed up?"

Mom tucked a loose strand of hair behind her ear. "I wouldn't describe this as dressed up."

"She's meeting Shorty at the diner," Rose said.

"It's just coffee." Mom waved her hand in the air.

"Rose, stop encouraging this thing with Shorty. It's going to be trouble."

Mom put her hands on her hips. "That's enough out of you, young lady!"

"Oh, really?" I shouted. "What about my freedom of speech?"

"If you keep this attitude, I'll revoke it!" Mom shouted back.

"Mom! Charlotte! Stop!" Rose said. "You're putting bad energy in the universe."

"The universe is overflowing with bad energy, and there's nothing you can do about it except keep it company! Haven't you figured that out yet?" Then I heard the door open and Freddy clomped down the stairs in his heavy boots. He wasn't wearing a hat, and there was a streak of blood on his face.

Our argument was forgotten. Mom, Rose, and I rushed toward him at the same time.

"What happened?"

"What's wrong?"

"Are you okay?"

He blinked back tears as he tore off his coat. He threw it in a heap by the refrigerator along with his boots.

"I'm fine."

"You don't look fine." Mom put her hands on his face. "Rose, be a love and get me a wet cloth."

Freddy pushed her hands away. "It's nothing."

"Where's your left hearing aid?" she asked.

He took a deep breath and released a sob. Mom hugged him and led him to the couch. Rose brought the cloth, and Mom wiped his face.

Mom said, "Charlotte, get my phone out of my purse

and reply to the text message from Shorty. Tell him I can't make it and I'll send him a message later."

I got the phone and typed, *Can't go tonight will send you a message later.* I got a glass of water and brought it to Freddy. "So what happened?"

Mom said, "A disturbed young man in the park threw snowballs at him. Look at his face."

"Bad Chad," Rose said.

"He took out my hearing aid. I didn't stop to pick it up. I just ran." Freddy looked ashamed. "Now it's ruined for sure."

"Maybe not," Rose said.

"He's right. It's ruined for sure," Mom said. "A few seconds in the snow is all it takes."

Freddy sighed. "I'm sorry."

"You don't need to be sorry." Mom squeezed his hand. "You did exactly what you needed to do. You got out of there. That was the right decision, honey."

"I know we can't afford to replace it."

"I'll talk to his parents."

"No! That'll make it worse," Freddy said. "I shouldn't have cut through the park. I figured it was too cold for him to be out there."

"You didn't do anything wrong," I said. "Bad Chad is awful."

Freddy looked surprised that I'd defend him after everything that had happened between us, but I didn't need Twin Superpowers to stand up for my brother.

"This was awful behavior, but it doesn't make him an awful person," she said. "I'll talk to his parents. Surely they'll pay for this."

Freddy said, "Mom! Are you kidding me? He is an awful person."

"Kids like Chad grow up in a negative and hostile environment, and that's what they project in the world." She patted Freddy's leg. "We'll go to Minneapolis Saturday and replace it. I'll set up a payment plan just in case, but hopefully his parents will take responsibility."

"Minneapolis? I can't wait to be in an actual city." I desperately needed to get out of Walnut Grove.

Mom gave me a stern look. "Freddy and I are going to Minneapolis. You and Rose will stay here and think about the problems you're having. Mia can keep an eye on you."

Rose looked at me. "Why are you in trouble?"

"Me? Why are you in trouble?"

Mom said, "It seems you're both missing assignments and being rude to your teachers."

Rose was missing assignments? Being rude to her teacher? Those homework-missing and rudeness genes belonged to me, not her. Everything was turned upside down.

"So we're grounded?" Rose asked.

"Not exactly. You're getting time to think affirming thoughts and redirect your energy."

In other words, we were grounded.

EIGHTEEN

Saturday morning, Mom and Freddy hit the road. Mom insisted we weren't grounded—just getting a concentrated period of time to think affirming thoughts—so we didn't feel guilty at all for going to the diner for lunch. Rose's Christmas money from Rey had finally arrived, and she was in a spending mood.

We sat in our favorite table by the window. Rose said, "Get anything you want. I have fifty dollars to spend."

"Fifty? You always get two hundred dollars at Christmas."

"Not this year," she said. "Dad said he needs to save money because his new wife is having a baby."

She said it like it was barely news, like she was filling the air with weather talk. Rose would have another sister, and I'd have a . . . what would I have? Stepsister? No, that didn't sound right. I'd have a half sister with a half sister or a half brother. My family was getting complicated.

"I don't know if I should say congratulations or I'm sorry."

"It's fine." She smiled. "Totally fine."

"Are you sure?"

"Hopefully I'll have another sister. Not as good as you. And I bet she'll be cute. Dad's wife is beautiful. He sent me a picture of her."

I couldn't make my words sound as happy as Rose's words, but I tried. "Good for you."

We decided to split chicken strips and fries so we'd be hungry enough for pie. After the waitress took our menus, Rose sipped her soda and asked, "So what's new at the museum?"

"It's a long story."

"Tell me."

"I don't feel like talking about it."

She crossed her arms. "You'd tell Freddy."

"Fine." I rolled my eyes. "It was a long day, you know? I got there early and overheard Gloria talking to Teresa, and she said something happened to their budget, and they're not going to pay Julia. And they said my online scrapbook is awful."

Rose's mouth dropped open. "That's so mean!"

"You know, at first I wanted to actually win that stupid

contest. I wanted to use the money to get another dog. It would've been for us, but mostly for you."

Her eyes filled with tears. "Really? That's so nice." She blew her nose in the napkin. "I've been sleeping with the Jack bag. Don't tell Mom. She'll think I'm being negative."

"What if the box inside the bag opens and you get ashes everywhere? That's gross."

"I'm careful. Besides, it wouldn't be all that gross. It's Jack."

"It's Jack's *ashes*."

"Maybe we can still get a dog. Maybe when Mom sells the Mars book."

"She can't even write the Mars book. Chances are she's not going to sell it." I felt bad for being such a rainbow-denier, but I couldn't help it. I waited for Rose to tell me that Mom would get a burst of inspiration and finish the book, and the book would be amazing, and the book would sell for lots of money, and then we'd have a real house and a dog, and the sun would shine every day, and flowers would grow in place of weeds, and every Sunday would be Christmas.

You know what she said?

Nothing. Not a word.

She ate exactly half of the chicken strips and fries and announced she wasn't in the mood for pie after all.

Just then Julia called. She never called, only texted, so I answered right away.

"Charlotte! We've got an emergency at the museum. Can you meet me there?"

"What's going on?"

"Gloria just called. A pipe burst in the back room. There's water all over. I'm on my way. Can you meet me now? Like right now?"

This wasn't my emergency. It wasn't Julia's emergency, either, but I hadn't told her yet about Gloria and Teresa and their budget problem.

"Charlotte?"

"I suppose." I huffed. "See you in a few."

I ended the call and rolled my eyes at Rose. "Emergency at the museum. You might as well come with."

After she paid the bill, we bundled up and crossed the highway. Rose tugged on my jacket. "What are you going to do?"

"Get in and out as fast as I can. Expect me to develop a headache."

"Should I get a headache, too?"

"Good idea."

"Wouldn't it be less suspicious if you got a headache and I got a stomachache?"

"Doesn't matter. After what they've done, I don't even care if they believe us."

I thought about how I'd felt when they'd said I was brilliant, how that feeling had kept me happily afloat for months. That feeling was a big, ugly lie. By the time we opened the museum door, my stomach was in knots. I had to take a few deep breaths to calm myself.

Julia came in behind us. "Hi guys. Where are Gloria and Teresa?"

"Five bucks says they're in the break room drinking coffee."

We went to the break room to hang up our gear, and, sure enough, those two gray-haired liars were sitting at the table sipping coffee. Some emergency.

"Hello, girls," Gloria said. "Cold enough for ya?"

"Definitely." Julia hung up her coat.

"And Rose came to help, too. What a sweetie." Teresa said the words so nicely it was almost like she believed them.

Rose looked at me and cleared her throat. "Yes, even though my stomach hurts very badly."

Julia was all business. "So what happened?"

"Thankfully the damage is all in the back room," Gloria said. "Everything back there we can replace—supplies for the bathroom, merchandise for the gift shop, and whatnot."

"Imagine if it had damaged the artifacts." Teresa put her hand on her heart.

"Imagine!" Gloria nodded.

They didn't care about Rose and her stomachache, obviously.

"What kind of merchandise?" Julia asked.

"We've got books, cookbooks, aprons, T-shirts, mugs,

postcards . . . some of it we can salvage. That's what I need you girls to do. Open all the boxes and sort what we'll need to toss and what we can clean up and sell in the shop."

"Insurance should cover the price of the lost merchandise," Teresa said.

"Good," I said. "It'd be awful if you had to use the money you owe Julia to pay for that."

I thought being a smart-mouth would burn off my anger, but it didn't. I felt even angrier. Gloria acted like she didn't hear me. Teresa said, "Anyhoo, we should get busy. Lots to do."

"I brought a special vacuum from home that sucks water." Gloria leaned against the counter. Apparently she planned to relax while we did all the work. "The carpet in the hallway is soaked. I'll show you how to use it."

I pressed my lips together to hold back my temper. It was Saturday. We weren't even scheduled to work. Julia said, "Basically we need to get rid of the water in the carpets and sort through the boxes for the gift shop. Is that right?"

"That's right," Teresa said. "There's water on the bathroom floor, too. Charlotte, I'll get you a mop."

Have you ever thought something in your head, and somehow the words slip out of your mouth?

Words you know should never be uttered?

That's what happened. I *thought*, "And what the heck are you going to do? Drink coffee?" And then I said it.

Rose gasped and slapped her hand over her mouth.

"Excuse me?" Gloria said.

"I'll be using the second vacuum," Teresa said. "Young lady, maybe it's okay to be rude to adults where you came from, but around here children respect their elders. Maybe your mother allows—"

"Don't blame my mom. Don't even talk about my mom."

"That's what happens when fathers aren't involved," Teresa said to Gloria. "Kids get no discipline, and they fall apart."

Julia's face went as red as mine felt, but she didn't say anything. Rose stood as frozen as Mount Rushmore. Even if I apologized, it wouldn't matter. My outburst would be all over town by morning. I pictured Gloria serving up chicken strips and gossip at the Prairie Diner, where kids eat free on Wednesdays, telling everyone I'd been a rude brat and it was my mom's fault. Why'd I ever think people in this town, especially these ladies, were nice?

"Sad state of affairs," Gloria said.

"You're cheaters! I hate this town, and I hate this museum!" I grabbed my coat and ran toward the door. "Come on, Rose!"

As I stepped outside, Rose at my heels, I turned and yelled one last thing into the building. "And yes, it's definitely cold enough for me!"

I ran as fast as heavy snow boots would carry me, past the fake sod house, past the replica church, toward the park. I hit a patch of ice, and my legs flew out from under me, and I landed on my back. It hurt, and I was glad. I had an excuse to cry.

. . . . .

It started snowing as soon as we got home. The radio said it wasn't going to be a heavy snowfall, but the winds were going to pick up and make driving difficult. Basically, it was a stupid typical winter day on the Minnesota prairie.

Rose made hot chocolate and turned on *The Hunger Games*. The movie had just ended when there was a knock on the basement door. We yelled, "Come in," and Julia came downstairs. I didn't feel like talking about the museum, but Julia needed to know the truth. When the story about my rudeness spread through town, I wanted people to at least know I had a reason—a good reason.

"What the heck happened back there?" Julia threw her arms in the air. "That was the most awkward thing ever, and I was stuck alone! Don't think I didn't want to run out behind you."

She looked mad, and I didn't blame her.

"You need to know the whole story," I said.

"My dad is going to be here any minute. I have to hang out with him tonight."

Our phone buzzed with a text. Rose said, "Mom says the roads are too bad to drive home. Mia is arranging for them to stay with her family."

"Ugh." I dropped to the couch in a heap. "The prairie hates us."

"Tell me quick," Julia said. "What happened?"

Rose said, "Charlotte was eavesdropping and—"

"Was not!" I said. "I accidentally overheard. There's a difference."

"Just hurry up," Julia said.

"I overheard Teresa and Gloria talking about a budget problem, and they said they wouldn't be able to pay you, and that our work wasn't good anyway."

"Are you serious?"

"That's what they said. I slipped away and waited for you. Then I said I had a headache and went home, because I didn't know what to do or say. So when I got there this morning, I was really mad, and then they were—"

"Bossing us around!" Julia said.

"And being totally lazy themselves," Rose said.

I nodded. "Exactly."

"No wonder you were mad." Julia crossed her arms. "When they said that stuff about single moms, I wanted to yell at them myself."

"We happen to have the greatest mom ever! Let's tell that to the gizzard ladies!" Rose said. "What happened after we left?"

"Gloria said Mrs. Newman got to help choose the winners of the essay contest. Gloria said your essay was terrible, but apparently Mrs. Newman said you're a deep thinker with a strong vocabulary. Something about knowing the difference between *literally* and . . . what's the word?"

"*Figuratively.*"

"Gloria said your essay was disrespectful to Laura. I guess Mrs. Newman said it was original and that you had great potential. Then Gloria said Mrs. Newman tricked her by saying she had an opportunity to turn you into a Laura fan."

Wow. Was anyone a better schemer than Mrs. Newman?

"So now what?" Rose said. "Julia, are you going to ask about getting paid?"

"Maybe I should wait for them to say something."

"Or should we talk to Mom and Mia?" Rose asked.

"They're just going to get upset," Julia said.

"But they'll make them pay you," Rose said.

"I don't want Charlotte to get in trouble for eavesdropping. I think we should wait for them to tell me I'm not getting paid. Then we can tell my grandmother and your mom."

As Julia and Rose debated a plan, I thought about Freddy. He was the one I talked to about stuff like this. Not Julia. Not Rose. I felt lonely. Without thinking, out of instinct, I said, "Maybe we should ask Freddy what he thinks."

Julia reached into her pocket for her phone. "Guys, I have to go. Grandma's texting me about Dad. I'll talk to you tomorrow."

Rose flopped onto the couch and crossed her arms as Julia headed upstairs. "That was a stupid thing to say."

"What?"

"About Freddy. He wasn't even there."

"Duh. But he might have an idea. That's all. There's no reason to make Mom stress out over this. She's already stressed out."

"Whatever," Rose grumbled. She pointed the remote at the TV and started the next *Hunger Games* movie.

While the movie played, I decided to do my homework. Mom was going to hear about my explosion at the museum. At least I better be able to show her I'd done my work. It was easy stuff, anyway. The worksheet for language arts was called "context clues." We had to figure out the meaning of underlined words in a sentence, which was pretty easy. I'd scribbled in most of the answers when the pen snapped and ink leaked on my fingers. I threw the pen away and got a pencil.

"Rose, you should do your late assignments. Let's not spend another weekend thinking positive affirmations and redirecting energy."

She didn't laugh. She didn't get my sense of humor at all.

I really missed Freddy, you know?

NINETEEN

When Mom and Freddy returned Sunday afternoon, Mom was frazzled. Normally the trip from Minneapolis to Walnut Grove took about three hours, but icy roads required slow speeds.

"We saw a dozen cars in the ditch between the city and here," Freddy said. "No joke."

Mom flopped onto the couch. "Please make me a cup of lemon tea. My whole body aches. My hands were glued to the steering wheel. My arms were tense. My back was tense. My shoulders were tense." Freddy warmed a cup of water in the microwave while Mom wrapped a blanket around herself. "I kept wondering how many pioneers died in the winter. They had no weather forecasts. They didn't have expensive winter gear to protect them from the cold. There was no way to call for help."

"People died in blizzards even when they were near their homes. They got lost going from the house to the barn," I said. "I read about it in those articles about pioneer life."

Freddy put a tea bag in the cup and handed it to Mom. She pulled a blanket over her lap and leaned her head back. "How was your Saturday?"

I said, "Let's just say there weren't a lot of positive affirmations."

"Oh boy," Mom said. "You'll have to fill me in."

"I'm starving," Freddy said. "Can I make a pizza?"

Rose handed Freddy his coat. "Forget the pizza. I took Charlotte out for lunch yesterday. It's your turn for a treat. We can have some Rose-and-Freddy time."

"I'm not in the mood."

"Come on! We've never gone to the diner just the two of us. We can split a chicken strip basket and then get dessert."

Freddy was going to refuse, but Mom's face made it clear he was going. "Such a generous offer. I am sure Freddy will accept graciously. Then Charlotte can tell me about the weekend."

Freddy wasn't thrilled, because he sort of huffed and puffed, but he put on his coat and they headed to the diner. Freddy and I used to roll our eyes when we were stuck with Rose, but she'd changed. Over the past few months, she spent a lot more time at home, so we'd been together constantly. I thought Rose had become less annoying. Maybe I was getting used to her. When I was little, I hated spaghetti, but it was on the weekly lunch rotation at every school we attended. Slowly I got a taste for it. Then I shocked Mom by ordering it at a restaurant.

But the opposite happened, too. Once I ate so many Twinkies I got sick. I never ate another Twinkie.

Was Rose spaghetti and Freddy a Twinkie?

I sat on the couch next to Mom. "Why didn't you tell us Rey and his wife are having a baby?"

Mom's face went white. "I had no idea! He told Rose?"

"Yes."

"We have a deal. He lets me know news first so I'm prepared to help Rose. What is going on with him? It's like he's so caught up in this woman he's forgetting his daughter."

I leaned against Mom's shoulder. She smelled like lemon tea and lavender oil. "Freddy's spreading bad energy, too. He's been weird. He's been mean, like not accepting Rose's invitation to lunch."

"Try to think of it this way: you and Freddy aren't growing apart, you're just growing up. You and Freddy were so close that it kept you from interacting with the world. It's good that you're starting to let other people in."

"I liked it the way it was."

"You can't stop change, so you might as well see the beauty in it."

197

"Will you please stop saying things like that?"

"It's my worldview." She smiled. "My children are but-terflies. Freddy is leaving the cocoon. Now it's your turn."

Someone knocked on the door. Before Mom had a chance to yell, "Come in," feet came down the stairs. Right away I could tell it was Mia because she always wore fuzzy blue slippers.

Then I saw her face. Her eyes were serious, almost pan-icked. "Martha, someone is here to talk to you."

A second set of legs appeared. It was a police officer. Mom tossed the blanket aside and jumped up. "What's wrong? What happened?"

"Are you Martha Lake?"

"Yes."

"I'm Officer Jeremy Otto. I'd like to ask your daughter a few questions."

My heartbeat went from normal to nuclear in one sec-ond. Mom crossed her arms. "Why on earth do you want to talk to Charlotte?"

The cop stared at me. "The Ingalls museum was vandal-ized. I'd like to know where your daughter was late last night."

TWENTY

I had to remind myself to take a breath, but Mom responded without a beat. "She was here in her bed!"

"Are you certain? Mrs. Ramos said you were away last night."

Mia said, "Now wait a minute, I had no idea something happened and—"

"What makes you think my daughter would do such a thing? She works at the museum, for goodness' sake."

The cop pulled a small notebook and pen from his pocket. "Apparently there was quite a dustup between her and the volunteers yesterday. I need to talk to potential suspects."

"My daughter is not a suspect!"

"It's true my mom was gone, but I never left the house

last night." I tried to sound firm and confident, but my voice shook.

Mia put her arm around me. "Charlotte is a wonderful girl. I wouldn't let her live in my house if I didn't trust her completely." I looked up at Mia. I had no idea she felt so strongly about me. I loved Mia so much at that moment.

But the cop was unmoved by Mia's declaration. "Charlotte, what happened after you left the museum?"

"I came home and watched movies with my sister. Julia came downstairs and talked to us. And we went to bed about ten. That's it."

Mom said, "If Charlotte had left the house, Mia and Miguel would've heard her."

"I think a person could walk up those steps and through the garage without people on the main floor hearing, especially at night," he said.

"I have excellent ears!" Mia said.

He ignored Mia and stared into my eyes, like he was trying to read my thoughts. "Charlotte, why did you yell at Gloria Johnson and Teresa Meadows?"

I swallowed hard. "Because they said my project was bad, and they said mean things about my mom."

"They didn't tell me that."

"See?" Mom said. "They're leaving out information."

He raised his eyebrows. "That certainly would give you a motive."

I was scared. I'd seen plenty of movies. When cops used the word *motive*, they were hauling someone to jail. He pointed to my hand. "What's that on your fingers?" I looked at the blotches of faded black ink, and before I could answer, he said, "Spray paint?"

"Ink! It's from a pen."

"The vandal used black spray paint." He said it like he'd just made the final guess in Clue. *Charlotte Lake in the Ingalls Museum with the spray paint.*

"But this is pen ink! I swear!"

"What size boots do you wear?"

"Leave right now." Mom marched toward him, completely unafraid. "Immediately. You cannot barge in here and accuse my child of crazy things."

The cop tucked the notebook into his pocket. "I'll give you folks some time to calm down. I'm writing a report. I've made note of the paint residue on her fingers and that she was unsupervised."

"Leave!" Mom shouted. Officer Otto gave the door a hard slam on his way out.

Mia put her arms around Mom. "It's okay. It'll be okay."

Mom hugged Mia, then came to me and put her hands on my shoulders. Mom looked into my eyes. "I will only ask you one time. Just once. Charlotte, did you do this thing?"

"No."

"That's all I need to hear."

Mia said, "Bundle up and meet me in the garage. We'll drive to the museum and see it for ourselves."

. . . . .

I gasped when I saw the black letters scrawled across the side of the building: *I hate Walnut Grove I hate Lara.*

Mia stopped the car. "Whoever did it doesn't know how to spell Laura." Then she pointed. "You can see the footsteps through the snow. That's why he asked you about your boot size."

"Everyone wears boots. It's winter. How many people in town have small feet? Probably two hundred. Probably more!" Mom said.

"Very true," Mia said. "I have small feet, and I'm an adult."

Mom looked at me in the back seat. "Start from the beginning. Tell me everything that happened."

Mia put the car in the park.

I told them about overhearing Teresa and Gloria talking about not having money to pay Julia. I told them how they said our work wasn't good. I told them that Julia came into the museum and that I said I had a headache and I left. I told them about getting the text about the water pipe breaking and how I went to the museum and lost my temper.

Mom sighed. "Why didn't you tell them you'd overheard their discussion, and what you heard upset you, and that you wanted them to explain what was going on?"

"Because I was mad and not thinking. I don't always have the perfect words. The words I had were *lazy* and *gossip.*"

"Oh dear," Mia said.

"I said I hated the museum."

"Oh dear," Mia said.

"This is why you need to choose your words more

carefully." Mom sank into the seat. "It's too late for that lecture. Besides, where would you get spray paint? You don't have access to that."

"Oh dear," Mia said.

"What?"

Mia pressed her lips together.

"Mia, what is it?" Mom's voice sounded urgent.

"We have spray paint in the garage."

"I didn't know that! I swear!"

In the rearview mirror, Mia's eyes, once so supportive, seemed to darken. Mom put her face in her hands and mumbled.

"What? Mom? What are you saying?"

"I need to drive. I just need to drive and drive and drive," she said. "Mia? Would you mind keeping an eye on Freddy and Rose today? Charlotte and I are going on a little road trip."

"But the roads are still icy."

"I don't care. I'll drive slow. I have to move. I can't sit here another second."

"Okay. I'll watch the kids."

The ugly words on the side of the museum faded from sight as we drove away. I'd moved all over the southeastern part of the country.

How could the six-block drive to Mia's house feel like the longest journey of my life?

Everything was different.

Everything was wrong.

· CHAPTER ·
TWENTY-ONE

From the air, I bet the highway looked like a gray ribbon woven into a white blanket. Every couple of miles we passed a farmhouse and its grove of trees, but mostly it was Mom and me and swirling snow. When the snow-covered prairie met the sky, the blue nearly burned with brilliance.

Mom said, "This highway is called the Laura Ingalls Wilder Historic Highway. That's what you'd call irony."

"I guess."

"If we stay on this road, we'll end up in De Smet, South Dakota, where the Ingalls family moved after Walnut Grove."

"Can we not stay on this road?"

Mom's laughter cut the tension, and my shoulders relaxed a little. The second I thought about Laura, the tension returned, only worse. I'd been accused of something I didn't do, but the feeling went deeper than that.

I felt bad for Gloria and Teresa, even though they were fake-nice, because there was nothing fake about how much they loved the museum.

But that wasn't the source of the tension, either. Everyone in Walnut Grove was proud of the town's history. When they drove by the museum and saw those ugly words, they'd feel angry and sad.

But that didn't explain my feelings, either. They went even deeper than that.

I realized I felt terrible for *Laura*. The family had had tough times in Walnut Grove. Pa couldn't pay the bills, the grasshoppers devoured all the crops, and Mary went blind. But after living on the lonely Kansas prairie, the Ingallses had found civilization in Walnut Grove. They had a real school, a nice church, and good neighbors. Laura's memories were happy. She loved splashing in Plum Creek and running barefoot through the prairie grasses. One Christmas, rich people in the East sent gifts to the church in Walnut Grove. Laura got a fur cape with a matching muff and a beautiful jewel box, which she kept her whole life. She loved it here, and when farming didn't work out, and they had to move for Pa's railroad job, she was really sad.

"Mom, I think I'm feeling Laura's energy—for real. She's sad about what happened to the museum."

"I feel it, too," Mom said.

"Whoever did it couldn't even spell her name. They're stupid and mean."

"Their behavior was stupid and mean. People aren't inherently stupid and mean. And *stupid* is a swear word. You shouldn't say it. Anyway, people are inherently good. I'll always believe that."

Not exactly a shocker, right?

I turned down the heater. My feet were sweating in my boots. I'd lived through months of winter, and I was still amazed I could sweat through the cold.

Mom wasn't thinking about the contradictions of winter weather. "If we get on the interstate, we could go west to Rapid City and into Wyoming and Montana. It would take us all the way to the Pacific coast." Mom used her dreamy, faraway voice, the voice that told me she was making plans to move.

"Why is everyone obsessed with going west?" My voice was so sharp that Mom took her eyes off the road for a moment to look at me. "The pioneers," I said. "But it's not just them. President Eisenhower started the interstate project in the 1950s to make it easier to get from coast to coast, like a modern transcontinental railroad."

"Sounds like someone's paying attention in school." Mom smiled. "There's something about our country and the West," she said in a dreamy voice. "It's romantic, and I don't mean in a boyfriend-girlfriend way, but we have this sense of pride in conquering the Wild West."

"When they built the railroad, men would ride the

trains with shotguns and kill buffalo just because it was fun, like an old-fashioned version of a video game."

"That's terrible," Mom said.

"Westward expansion stunk if you were Native American."

"I know."

Mom and I pulled down our visors and blinked against the brightness. The sun was dropping into the horizon, big and fat and lazy, curling up in its earth bed. "I can't drive west with the sun like that. It's killing my eyes. Let's find a place to eat."

Mom turned the car around and drove to Marshall. We stopped at a bar and grill downtown and ordered a chicken strip basket to share. I knew I wouldn't eat much. My stomach rumbled from hunger, but I couldn't imagine swallowing anything.

"What's going to happen, Mom?"

"Honestly, we're almost out of money. That Chad kid's mother was not helpful. Shorty tracked down her cell phone number, and I called her Saturday afternoon. She refuses to pay and even denies Chad threw the snowball. Shorty says I should take them to small claims court, but I'm ready to be done with all of this. I'm thinking we could go to Arizona. It'd be warm in the winter and a new environment will feed my creativity. Plus, I have to get a job, and what is there in Walnut Grove for work? Waitressing at the diner?"

"I want you to finish the book. We all do."

"The problem with the book is the science. It's too complicated. I can't make it work, so I came up with this idea. Instead of science fiction, I'll make it a fantasy novel. Then I can make up anything. It doesn't have to be rooted in science."

"So a fantasy novel about kids on Mars?"

"Exactly. Maybe they get to Mars on a dragon."

How do you tell someone her ideas are like broccoli-flavored cereal? They don't go together.

You don't. You nod, which is what I did.

She sipped her coffee. "I thought we should finish the school year before we leave, but with this museum thing hanging over our heads, we should just go." She looked sad for a moment. "Freddy is going to be very angry."

I didn't want to feel bad for Freddy, but I did. He got to be a rock star for a couple months, and it wouldn't be easy to leave Red Fred behind.

"He has a lot of friends," I said. "Like literally everyone is his friend."

"He can stay in touch with them. They can be friends for life."

"Like me and Molly Smith?"

Mom thought a minute. "That name is familiar. Who's Molly Smith?"

"She was the first, best, and only friend I ever had. And we were going to write to each other, and it never happened. Not even once."

"Why didn't you write to her?"

I wasn't surprised she didn't remember. I said, "It was when you lost all your contacts. She promised she would send me a letter, but she never did." My eyes stung with tears. "She lied to me. She forgot all about me."

"I'm so sorry, honey." Mom leaned closer to me. "But you don't know that she forgot."

"Yes, I do. I never got a letter. And I never sent one because I couldn't."

"Maybe the same thing happened to her. She could've lost our contact information. Or maybe the mail carrier lost the letter or delivered it to the wrong apartment. Maybe when I brought in the mail, it slid out of my hands. Maybe it accidentally got put on a stack of paper we threw away. Maybe she wrote to you *after* we moved. We only stayed in that apartment three months." I wiped my eyes with a napkin and blew my nose. "Charlotte, don't think for a second that she forgot you. Because, my dear, you are unforgettable."

I shrugged.

"We all assume things," Mom said. "It's human nature. But I want you to promise me you will assume good things first. Not bad things."

"You really think the letter got lost?"

"It's much more likely than her forgetting you or lying." Mom squeezed my hand. "It's entirely possible that Molly is somewhere right now—maybe Utah, maybe Maine— and she's talking to her mom about you. She's sharing a wonderful memory. That's how the universe works. You two are connected forever. Do you feel the spark right now?"

I paused, waiting for the spark.

Nothing. Not even a tingle.

Was it worth telling her no?

Probably not.

"I'll try to feel the spark later, okay? Mom, I don't think Freddy is going to see it your way. He has more than twenty Mollys. Besides, if we leave now, everyone will think we're running away because I vandalized the museum."

"Life isn't about what you're running from, it's about what you're running toward. Make sense?"

"Not even a little."

"I don't care what other people think. You know you didn't do it. I know you didn't do it. Anyone who knows you knows you didn't do it."

"That's the problem, Mom. Nobody knows me. Only you and Freddy and Rose know me. Nobody in the whole world really knows me."

I figured the conversation was getting to her because she started chewing on her fingernail. She wasn't a nail chewer. Finally she said, "Can you try to think of it like this? You get to reinvent yourself every time you move. That was the exciting part about moving when I was a kid and my father was in the military. I'd pick someone new to be in each place we lived. Once I was a Goth kid. I wore black every single day. Sometimes I'd be the smart kid.

In Atlanta, I joined the drama club. In Boston, I played volleyball and hung out with all the jocks."

"I don't want to be reinvented. I don't even know how to do that. I'm . . . I'm . . ." I searched for the words to describe myself. "I'm me. Just me."

Mom stared out the window until the waiter brought the bill.

. . . . .

When we got home, Freddy and Rose were already in bed. I scrubbed my fingers until they ached to get rid of the ink stains. I was exhausted, but I couldn't sleep. I told myself Monday would be fine. Everyone had learned about the vandalism Sunday, but the name of the prime suspect probably wouldn't spread until Tuesday, maybe even Wednesday. I must have drifted off to sleep because suddenly Freddy was tapping my shoulder.

He whispered, "Come out to the living room so we can talk."

Before I even sat down on the couch he was asking questions. "What happened? What's going on?" You'd think his voice would be like, *My poor sister, how can I help?* But it wasn't. His voice was like, *What did you do?*

"I don't know what happened."

He didn't need Twin Superpowers to know I was innocent.

Right?

I was a person he'd known for twelve years, a person who'd never broken a law or any rules other than staying up too late or not doing my homework. Yes, I snorted and sighed, and sometimes I assumed bad things first, but I was not a vandal or a destroyer. Not now. Not ever.

"I have friends for the first time in my life, and now everyone's going to think we're a bunch of criminals."

I swallowed and straightened my shoulders. "I didn't do it."

"One of the cans of spray paint is missing from the garage."

"You obviously need your second hearing aid, because I said I didn't do it."

"The cops think you did and now everyone is going to think we're bad people."

I sprang off the couch. "Freddy, if I had decided to spray-paint the museum, you know what I would've written? *I hate Red Fred.*"

I marched into my room and slammed the door. I didn't care if the noise woke up everyone in the house.

· PART THREE ·

On the Banks of Dumb Creek

· CHAPTER ·
TWENTY-TWO

I got ready for school but waited in the bedroom until I heard Freddy and Rose say good-bye to Mom. Then I put on my gear and grabbed a granola bar to eat while I walked.

Mom hugged me. "Everything will be fine."

"I'm trying to assume a good thing. Maybe they caught the real criminal overnight."

Mom's face didn't look optimistic. "Charlotte, we have to face the possibility that the cop has already made up his mind. His energy was entirely negative."

Then I got a brilliant idea. I burrowed in the trash and picked through pizza wrappers, tissues, and a bag of microwave popcorn. "Charlotte . . . ," Mom said like she thought I was losing my mind.

Finally I found the leaky pen. "See this pen? The black

stuff on my hands was ink. You have to call that cop and tell him."

Mom sighed. "I don't know, hon. The cop could say you broke the pen after the fact as a way to explain why you had black stains on your fingers. I think this is a man who looks for guilt, not a man who looks for innocence."

"I should've showed you when he was here, but I didn't think about it."

She took the pen and dropped it back in the trash. "Forget the pen." Then she put one hand on each of my shoulders and turned me so I was facing her. "Charlotte, you're the bravest person I know."

"Really?" I was afraid to look her in the eye.

"'You are braver than you believe, stronger than you seem, smarter than you think.' Do you know who said that?"

"Laura Ingalls?"

"No."

"Dr. Seuss?"

"No. Winnie the Pooh." I looked up. She was smiling. She hugged me again. "Remember I believe in you."

"Thanks, Mom."

. . . . .

I barely slid into my desk before the bell rang. One by one, heads turned and looked at me—everyone except Freddy, who stared at his notebook. How could they know already? It'd been one day. One! Maybe I was paranoid.

Mom says if you look hard enough for something, you'll find it. I took out my folder and a note someone had stuck in my desk fell to the floor. It said, *Hey Lara, spell much? You must live on the Banks of Dumb Creek!*

I knew people would hear right away that the museum had been vandalized. If you drove through town, you'd see it. But it should've taken at least two days for everyone to know I'd been accused. The school building had been open only thirty minutes, and already the kids in my class knew.

I avoided eye contact, including Julia and Emma and Bao. I remembered what Julia had said about Emma and Bao having her back when everyone gossiped about her after the robbery at Shorty's gas station.

Would they have my back now?

I didn't want to take the risk. Because if the answer was no, if they didn't have my back, I would literally collapse. I couldn't take one more slap right now.

Mrs. Newman was about to speak when a voice came over the intercom. "Mrs. Newman, please send Charlotte Lake to the office."

Have you ever been paged to the office?

It was the most humiliating moment of my existence. It was the opposite of being invisible. My face flushed red. Heads turned; people stared. Without making eye contact, I left the classroom and walked to the office as slowly as possible. I considered hiding in the bathroom, but eventually they'd come looking for me. It was better to face Mr. Crenski and tell him what I'd told the police officer.

The secretary gave me a cold look when I entered. She pointed to Mr. Crenski's office. "He's waiting for you."

Everyone in school laughed about Mr. Crenski's size. He was shorter than all the teachers. In a town of ironic nicknames, Mr. Crenski's friends probably called him Giant. But he didn't feel short to me. His energy felt big and angry and mean. As I waited for him to finish his phone call, I replayed Mom's words over and over. *The bravest person. The bravest person. The bravest person.* Finally he hung up.

"It sounds like there was trouble over the weekend."

I nodded.

"So you're aware of the situation."

I nodded.

"Charlotte, I want you to understand my goal is to help kids who get into trouble, not to hurt them. I want you to understand that I didn't call you in here to yell at you or frighten you. Okay?"

"Okay."

"It's a small town, and people talk. The best way to stop the talking is to settle the mystery. People have short memories. Life returns to normal quickly. Does that make sense?"

It made zero sense, but I nodded again.

"People understand that kids make mistakes. Adults understand that kids don't have the wisdom and coping skills to deal with intense feelings. Make sense?" His voice sounded soft and reasonable, but his energy was still big and angry and mean.

"I guess so."

"Why were you angry at the museum ladies?"

"I was angry, but I didn't—"

"One step at a time. Let's just focus on the museum. Did you manage to get a key to the museum door?"

"I don't understand."

"A reasonable person might wonder if the pipe sprung a leak or if it was intentionally loosened. I'm not making conclusions, but it's a reasonable question, don't you think?"

I saw where this was going. They thought I'd spray-painted the building *and* caused the flooding. I shivered from my head to my toes. There was a knock at the door, and before Mr. Crenski could answer, Mrs. Newman stepped inside.

"Is there something you need?" Mr. Crenski asked.

"I came to see if Charlotte's mother was here, and the secretary told me she hasn't been called. So I thought it would be appropriate, perhaps, for me to be here." She didn't use her fake smile, or her fake-nice voice.

"I appreciate your offer, but you need to be in your classroom." Mr. Crenski didn't fake smile, either.

"This district has a policy that kids cannot be questioned about a crime without a parent present. I assigned my other students silent reading time, and Mrs. Vinton has first hour free, so she agreed to keep an eye on them."

"This district also has a policy that teachers shouldn't be insubordinate with the principal."

"Martha Lake needs to be here."

Mrs. Newman was standing up for me—me, Charlotte Lake, the new kid, the kid she knew would be gone in a blink. The kid who lied to her. And didn't do her assignments on time. She knew, and she confronted Mr. Crenski anyway.

"This isn't a formal procedure," he said. "I'm simply letting Charlotte know that telling the truth is important, and the consequences of admitting a crime are not severe. The consequences of *not* admitting a crime, however, are severe."

"I see." Mrs. Newman let the silence draw out before saying, "We also need to let Charlotte know that it's a lie to say you committed a crime just because adults are pressuring you to do so."

Mr. Crenski's face burned red. "Obviously."

"As Charlotte's teacher, I would like you to do one of two things. Call Martha Lake and speak to Charlotte in her presence, or send Charlotte back to class with me."

Mr. Crenski shuffled some papers on his desk before clearing his throat. "Very well. Charlotte may return to class." The tone in his voice said he was madder at Mrs. Newman than at me.

I followed Mrs. Newman back to the classroom. She stopped outside the door to talk to me. "Did you bring a lunch today?"

"No. I figured you wouldn't let me."

"If you're willing to stay in the classroom and talk, I'll

have the cafeteria bring us trays. I have something to show you."

Then she turned on her heel and led me back to class.

.   .   .   .   .

When everyone left for lunch, Mrs. Newman got on her phone and ordered two lunch trays. She pulled a piece of paper from a folder and handed it to me. It was a letter from my teacher in Lexington.

To Whom It May Concern:

I rarely write a formal letter to include with a student's records, but in the case of Charlotte Lake, I believe it's warranted.

Charlotte joined my classroom in November. Her test scores from her previous districts were average as were the assessments completed by my district. Her classroom work met minimum standards. She had no discipline problems. She did not participate in classroom discussion unless she was required to do so.

My students are required to keep a free-writing journal. They are given time to write each day and encouraged to write at home as well. They can write about anything they want, from poetry to short stories to reactions to classroom lessons or current events. I don't read the entries or grade them, because the purpose is simply to encourage private writing and reflection, but I do occasionally check to make sure they're writing.

At the end of the year, I discovered Charlotte's journal in her desk. I was astounded by what I read. Charlotte, my most average student, could write far beyond her grade level. She wrote poetry, short stories, and reflections of life at home and school. I was impressed by not only the quality of the writing, but also the depth of her thinking. For example, we studied Kentucky's government and had a discussion about the importance of voting. That week, Charlotte wrote her reaction to the discussion. She made a compelling case that the emphasis on "getting out the vote" was misplaced. She argued that voters should be urged to learn about the issues and the candidates. If the voters weren't willing to make informed decisions, she said, they should be urged to not vote.

Charlotte came to me late in the year. I had thirty-two students and no assistant in my classroom, not even a single parent volunteer. It's with deep regret that I'm about to use a cliché: Charlotte slipped through the cracks.

I hope you're able to do what I was not: connect with Charlotte and tap her potential.

Sincerely,
Jane Alton

I had to read it twice to believe it. I'd figured if Mrs. Alton thought of me at all, and I was sure she didn't, it was because I sat by Big Nose Girl, who didn't speak English well. Mrs. Alton always had to help her, and the room was crowded. Mrs. Alton could barely squeeze between our desks, and she always apologized for bumping into me. To her, I was Girl in the Back Row.

Who knew teachers were so observant?

I gave the paper to Mrs. Newman. "I'm not sure what I'm supposed to say."

"I want you to know there are people in your corner." Her eyes were softer.

"Are you going to ask me what happened at the museum?"

"Is there something you want to tell me?"

A lunch lady came in and put trays of tater tot hot dish in front of us. Mrs. Newman wrinkled her nose when she took a bite. I said, "I was snotty to Gloria and Teresa, but I didn't damage the pipes, and I didn't paint on the building. I overheard them saying bad things about the project I'm doing."

"So you're guilty of rude behavior?"

"Very guilty," I said. "But now it looks like I have a reason for vandalizing the building."

Mrs. Newman nodded. "In television shows they call that a motive."

"I know I wrote a negative essay, but I was mad when I wrote it. I've spent a couple months in Laura's world. I like her. I gave my family cups, sticks of candy, and pennies for Christmas, just like the Christmas in *Little House on the Prairie*. Maybe the person who did it doesn't even hate Laura Ingalls. Maybe they just wanted to destroy something that makes other people happy."

"Unfortunately, there are people like that in the world."

I put a mushy tater tot in my mouth. I could barely swallow it. I'd only eaten a few bites of a granola bar that morning, but my stomach felt as full as Thanksgiving.

"I'd like us to discuss the Trail of Tears article this week. Would you be up for that?"

"During lunch?"

"Sure." She sighed. "But you will have to face the kids at some point. The longer you wait, the harder it's going to be. And if they don't hear anything from you, they're going to jump to conclusions."

"Okay."

"This hot dish tastes as bad as it looks."

"You should try the hamburgers. They're the worst."

"I'll take your word for it."

There was something I wanted her to know. "Mrs. Newman?"

"Yes?"

"My mom and I drove by the museum and saw the spray paint, and I can tell you this: I can spell Laura. The person who did it can't."

She nodded. "Excellent point."

. . . . .

As soon as the bell rang, I raced to my locker, grabbed my stuff, and bolted out the door. I couldn't look into the eyes of my friends—or anyone. I put on my winter gear when I got outside of school and ran all the way home. Mrs. Newman was right. I'd have to face everyone eventually, but I was going to put it off as long as possible.

Mom had a cup of hot chocolate waiting for me. "How did it go?"

"It could've been worse. I stayed in class for lunch." I thought about telling her about Mr. Crenski but decided to hang on to that information. Mom might call and yell at him, and it could be worse for me.

She squeezed my shoulder like she was preparing me for news, apparently because she was. "Honey, you need to know the police officer stopped by and asked if I would consent to a formal interview with you at the sheriff's office. Then he gave me this." She handed me a piece of paper. My Laura Ingalls essay. The essay that described why Laura Ingalls was ruining my life. "This doesn't help your case."

"Are they even considering it could've been someone else?"

She took a deep breath. "I want to make sure you understand that you can tell me anything, if there's anything to tell, and I will help you."

"You want to know if I did it? You said you believed me!" I stood up so fast I knocked my chair over and stormed into my room, but she was right behind me.

"Charlotte, I do believe you. But it's important for you to know if you do something wrong—this weekend, next year, when you're thirty years old—I'll be there to support you."

I flopped onto the bed. "Whatever."

"Look, I think you agree that you were rude to Gloria and that other woman."

"Teresa."

"It'd create some good will if you wrote them a letter apologizing for your behavior."

"They should apologize to me and Julia. They're not going to pay her. Is that fair?"

"No, it's not. Even so, you should react to an injustice in a way that demonstrates the beautiful heart I know you have."

"Are you sure my heart is beautiful?"

"I see it every single day."

I started to cry. "I'm afraid."

Mom couldn't find any tissues, so she brought a roll of toilet paper from the bathroom. I cried and wiped tears and blew my nose until I didn't have anything left. I leaned against Mom and fell asleep and didn't wake until morning.

TWENTY-THREE

We had a substitute teacher Tuesday—an old lady named Mrs. Lester. Her eyes and face were so mean she made Mrs. Newman seem like a puppy. Mrs. Lester looked like she had once had plump cheeks, and they'd drooped over time and hung like water balloons against her neck. She said she retired from teaching "a long, long time ago," which told me she wasn't old enough to have known Laura Ingalls, but she was definitely from the time when teachers smacked kids with rulers. Obviously she wasn't the kind of teacher who would eat lunch with me. Mrs. Newman had picked a terrible time to be sick.

I got my folder out of my desk, and someone had taped a piece of paper to it that said, *Sorry about the note from yesterday. Ethan.* Weird. This new note probably had nothing to do with me. He probably meant to give it to someone else and put it in my desk by mistake. There's no way Ethan was admitting he wrote the mean note and was actually apologizing for it.

Right?

I mean, why would he do that?

I crushed the paper into a ball and stuffed it in my pocket. I kept my eyes locked on the front of the room. I was afraid to look at Bao and Emma, because if they weren't giving me sympathetic looks, if they didn't smile at me or sigh or shake their heads like *I'm so sorry*, my heart would explode.

Mrs. Lester looked at Mrs. Newman's class notes and said, "It appears you're supposed to be working in teams on a science project." She shook her head. "Children, this business of group work means one thing: a couple of good kids do all the work, and the rest of the lazy ninnyhammers do nothing. If we're going to break into teams, we'll drill with math flashcards." She looked at Chuck and said, "Where are the math flashcards?"

Like the Asian boy should know?

Chuck shrugged.

"Never mind." She sighed. "I'll think of something else. Everyone can read until I come up with an appropriate lesson plan."

I felt eyes looking at me all morning, and I swore I heard Obviously Popular Girl—those popular girls are meaner than snakes—whisper my name to Greasy Hair

Boy. I watched Mrs. Lester all morning like she was the only person in the room. Making eye contact with Obviously Popular Girl would be an invitation for her to strike.

After everyone left for lunch, I got my sandwich and returned to my desk. I knew she'd send me to the lunchroom, but it was worth trying. Sure enough, Mrs. Lester said, "What are you doing?"

"I always eat lunch in here and get caught up on work."

"I'm going to the teachers' lounge. You can't stay here alone. Take your lunch to the cafeteria."

She was holding a ruler, so I didn't argue. I took my lunch to the bathroom and ate my cheese sandwich in a stall. I heard the door open and a couple girls talking. It sounded like Tallest Girl in Class and Obviously Popular Girl.

The water turned on and off, and Tallest Girl in Class said, "It's totally unfair. It's not Mrs. Newman's fault."

"Do you think she'll get fired?"

"I don't know. My mom said suspended. Is that the same as fired?"

Suspended? Fired? Mrs. Newman wasn't sick?

"All because of Charlotte. I hope she's happy."

What the heck?

What did I have to do with any of this?

It took a few seconds for it to sink in.

Mrs. Newman wasn't sick. She was in trouble for helping me with Mr. Crenski! The cheese sandwich gurgled in my stomach. I felt like puking. The door opened, and their

voices faded away. Now there were two people in trouble—
Mrs. Newman and me—and neither of us had done anything wrong. Mom was right. The cops weren't looking for
other suspects. They had me, and their work was done. As
far as I could tell, there was only one way out of this mess.

I had to figure out who did it.

But who would be mad at the Laura Ingalls Wilder
Museum?

Me, of course.

But who else?

Think, Charlotte, think!

Suddenly Julia's face flashed in my mind. Saturday
afternoon I told her they'd trash-talked our project and
that she wasn't getting paid.

She wasn't getting paid! At least I wasn't losing money.
Logically she should be even madder than me. And she probably knew her grandparents had spray paint in the garage.

All the pieces of the puzzle snapped together. I waited
for the hall to clear out after the bell rang. Then I marched
to the office. I was going to tell Mr. Crenski to give his
little speech about honesty to Julia. I'd have a hundred
apologies by the end of the week. Red Fred's popularity
would be secure. People wouldn't judge my single mom.
They'd judge Julia and her single mom.

They'd judge Julia and her single mom.

I stopped with my hand on the office door. I heard
Mom's voice. *Assume good things.*

I had thought Julia was fake-nice. But she was actually nice.

I had thought Julia was Nellie Oleson. But she was the anti-Nellie.

Julia was proud of our work—too proud to do anything to the museum. She was kind and funny. Most of all, Julia was my friend.

I knew Julia. After the trouble when her dad had robbed Shorty's gas station, there's no way she'd risk . . .

Wait a minute!

Her dad!

Why hadn't I thought of it sooner?

Her dad was a criminal. He was visiting Julia that night. He had access to the garage. As for a motive, well, obviously Julia had told him the museum ladies weren't going to pay her. And he got mad.

Everything made sense. Julia's dad was a thief and a vandal. His guilt would be hard for Julia. She'd be the source of gossip again, but Emma, Bao, and I would have her back. Besides, she hated her dad. She didn't even want to visit him. It's not like she'd be surprised.

Without another thought, I went into the office and asked the secretary if I could talk to Mr. Crenski. Five minutes later, I was in his office.

Mr. Crenski clasped his hands together. "So you have something to tell me."

I swallowed hard. "I didn't want to say anything before

because Julia is my friend, and she's the nicest girl in school, but—"

"Charlotte, you need to think long and hard before you tell me Julia Ramos vandalized the museum."

"No! Not Julia. Her dad. Did you know he robbed the gas station?"

"Everyone in Walnut Grove is familiar with her father."

"He was visiting Julia the night the museum was vandalized."

"You had spray paint on your fingers."

"It was ink!"

I knew then he'd already made up his mind about me. If I didn't act fast, I was going to be the guilty one. I opened my mouth and let the words tumble out. "In the middle of the night, I heard noises coming from the garage. I tiptoed up the stairs and when it was quiet, I opened the door. The garage was empty, so I figured it was just my imagination. Just to be sure, I went to the door that leads to the driveway. There's a small window in that door, so I looked outside and saw Julia's dad getting into his car, and he was holding something that looked like a can. I didn't know what it was. I figured it was no big deal, so I went to bed."

Mr. Crenski's face revealed nothing. He tapped a pen on his desk and thought for a minute. "Why are you coming forward with this now? It seems convenient that you reveal this information only after you've been questioned."

"I know it looks that way." My heart beat like a snare

drum. "I didn't want Julia to go through all that stuff with her dad again, because it was hard for her, and she's been so nice to me. I figured the whole thing would just blow over, and none of the kids would ever know I'd been accused. I didn't know people would actually believe I'd sneak out of the house in the middle of the night, when it's freezing cold and pitch-black, and walk six blocks *all by myself* and write on the building. I know how to spell Laura, and it's not L-A-R-A."

All true, right?

He rubbed his chin. "It's a crime to vandalize a building, but it's a much worse crime to falsely accuse someone of a crime or to lie to police. Do you understand that?"

I nodded.

"I'll call the sheriff's office. Will you tell him what you told me?"

My heart beat even faster. I was sweating. "Yes."

"All right."

"Does that mean Mrs. Newman will be back tomorrow?"

"That's private information, Charlotte. You can go to class now. The secretary can give you a pass."

You'd think the weight on my shoulders would float away like a balloon.

But it didn't float away. It felt heavier.

Maybe I was right about Julia's dad.

Or maybe I'd just assumed the worst thing.

Again.

News traveled at the speed of light in Walnut Grove. Right before bedtime, when I was reading in my room, I heard Julia ask Mom if she could talk to me. I'd been expecting her, and I'd planned what I was going to say. I wouldn't deny it. I'd tell her exactly what I'd told Mr. Crenski—that I didn't say anything right away because I wanted to protect her. She'd like me for that.

Julia barged into my room, and before I could say a word, she hissed, "Why did you tell Mr. Crenski stuff about my dad?"

"I didn't want to, but I didn't have a choice. They wouldn't stop blaming me."

"Well, now they won't stop blaming him, and he swears he didn't do it. And I believe him."

I didn't expect her to believe him. "I thought you hated your dad."

"I don't hate my dad. Sometimes I don't like him very much, but I don't hate him. Everything finally calmed down, and he swore to me he'd never get in trouble again. He doesn't drink anymore. Now it's a mess again, and it's because of you!"

"I don't want it to be a mess for either of us." My voice cracked, and I blinked back tears.

Julia sat on Rose's bed and crossed her arms. "Why didn't you tell me so at least I knew what was coming?"

"I guess I didn't have a chance."

"Gloria will probably fire me."

"They weren't going to pay you anyway."

"I'm mad about that, but I really liked working there. I thought we were part of something really cool, Charlotte. We were making memories for every person who ever visits the museum. Thousands of people."

My stomach clenched tight. "I know."

"Dad was fine that night. He didn't even argue with Grandpa. He's on probation, so if he's guilty, he'll go to jail, probably for a long time."

My heart was beating hard again. My big idea had backfired. I didn't know he'd go to jail for vandalism. It was a crime, but not a big-deal crime. But if Julia's dad didn't do it, then who did?

Julia started crying. "Are you sure it was my dad?" she asked. "I mean, you've never seen my dad. He's not Hispanic, you know. His last name is Swenson."

I never thought about what Julia's dad looked like. I figured the fact that he'd been in Walnut Grove that night would be enough evidence. I needed to buy myself some time to think instead of letting the words tumble out. "Hold on. I'll get you some tissues." I got a roll of toilet paper from the bathroom, and when I touched the doorknob, I got a shock. A big one. It was so big it sparked an idea. A better idea than accusing Julia's dad.

I handed Julia the tissue for her nose and said, "I assumed it was your dad because he'd been visiting. But by any chance, does he look like Bad Chad?"

Julia leapt from the bed. "No! Not at all! My dad is short and chubby."

"Well, this guy was tall and thin like Bad Chad."

"Oh my God!" Her face lit up. "It was Bad Chad! He probably got into the garage through the door from the backyard. My grandparents forget to lock it all the time. Charlotte, we have to call the police right now."

"It's late. Let's figure it out tomorrow, okay?"

"I have to tell my grandparents. They immediately believed it was my dad. Immediately! I'm so mad at them! So much for innocent until proven guilty."

"I know!"

Who cared about Bad Chad? He was rotten to the core. He smoked. He tormented kids. He hurt Freddy. He stuck my mom with a bill she couldn't afford to pay. Even if Bad Chad didn't do it—and obviously he did—everyone knew he'd eventually be a professional criminal. Somewhere there was a jail cell with his name on it.

It's karma, right?

TWENTY-FOUR

There were no notes in my desk the next day.

I allowed myself to look at Bao. She waved hello.

Then I took a deep breath and allowed myself to glance at Emma. She smiled.

Noah even called me Gazelle.

News definitely traveled fast in Walnut Grove.

Then Mrs. Lester announced that kids these days rely on computers for spelling, which was a terrible problem in education, so she was going to hold an old-fashioned spelling bee.

"I've read the lesson plan from front to back, and I don't see any mention of spelling tests." She shook her head and sighed. "I hope the taxpayers never find out."

We stood side by side against the wall of windows.

Mrs. Lester pointed to a student and called out a word. They were easy at first. *Proven. Declare. Machine.* A few kids were knocked out by *niece, neighbor,* and *definite.* Katie Turner botched *business.* B-U-S-N-E-S-S. I could tell she was nervous. Then the words got harder. *Carnival. Squirrel.* Freddy was a terrible speller. He blew *parachute.* P-A-R-A-S-H-O-O-T. Julia dropped out because she said E-N-T instead of A-N-T on *defiant.* Then Noah bombed museum. M-U-S-U-E-M.

Mrs. Lester shook her head and crossed her arms. "Someday you'll need to type a memo to your boss, and you won't know how to spell a simple word like *museum.* What will you do then?"

Noah shrugged. "I guess I'll use spell check."

"And who checks the spell checker?"

The question was so crazy nobody answered. Noah looked relieved when he sat down.

Normally, I'd blow it at that very moment. Even though I was a great speller—once I saw a word, it stuck in my head—my plan would be to drop out exactly halfway through. Not too smart, not too stupid. But this time, I couldn't bear to stop in the middle.

I was thinking about that day in Marshall, after the police officer came to the house, when Mom had said she'd liked to reinvent herself when she moved as a kid. She'd tried out being a smart kid and a Goth kid and a drama kid.

And me?

I'd been the same invisible version of myself in every place I've ever lived.

Aside from Freddy, only Julia, Emma, and Bao knew anything about me, because I'd been hiding. My classmates were hearing more from me during a spelling bee than they had during the entire year. I didn't need to invent anything. I could try just being me.

Right?

Mrs. Lester looked at me. *"Influence."*

Those words that could be either *ence* or *ance* were tricky. But I knew this one for sure. "I-N-F-L-U-E-N-C-E."

Next Mrs. Lester knocked out Chuck with *arrogance.*

Soon it was down to Bao and me. When Bao said "A-N-C-E" instead of "E-N-C-E" for *correspondence*, I was the last student standing.

Mrs. Newman would be proud.

But Mrs. Lester said to me, "You're the winner, but don't get cheeky. It's not like you had much competition."

Those words were daggers. I felt hot from head to toe. I cleared my throat and said, "I can do more."

"Excuse me?"

"I know lots of words because of Mrs. Newman." I sounded ridiculous, but nobody laughed. The room was quieter than a library on Friday night. Twenty-plus pairs of eyes stared at me like I was a stranger. I was going to show them who I was. Smart kid. Innocent kid. Charlotte Lake, great speller and champion of Mrs. Newman, the only person who had championed me.

Sounds crazy, right?

I didn't care. It felt like freedom.

Mrs. Lester squinted and said, "Is that so? Let's see, then. *Sophomore.*"

"S-O-P-H-O-M-O-R-E."

"Questionnaire."

Two Ns? Or one? I looked at Freddy. He leaned forward, pressed his lips together, and stared at me, like he was cheering me on. I didn't feel our Twin Superpowers fire up, not at all, but I didn't need them. Not for spelling. I imagined the word as though it were in a book. "Q-U-E-S-T-I-O-N-N-A-I-R-E."

"Advantageous."

"A-D-V-A-N-T-A-G-E-O-U-S."

She smiled wickedly, like she was about to nail me. "A final word for you, Cheryl."

"It's Charlotte."

"A final word for you, Charlotte. See if you can define it and spell it." Mrs. Lester paused for effect.

I closed my eyes and thought of Mom. She'd tell me to open myself up to the universe and ask for help. That's what I tried to do. I didn't have crystals or essential oils. I couldn't drop to the floor and get in a yoga pose. But I had my mind, so I asked Laura for help—Laura because she competed in spelling bees for entertainment and Laura because she once stood up to a teacher who was mean to her sister. Mom said the one advantage to being dead is the ability to understand the living. Laura knew I didn't wreck her museum.

Mrs. Lester crossed her arms and spit out a word. *"Transcontinental."*

I whispered, "Thank you, Laura." With a booming voice, in front of all my classmates, I said, *"Transcontinental* means extending across a continent. T-R-A-N-S-C-O-N-T-I-N-E-N-T-A-L."

Mrs. Lester scowled.

You know who clapped and stomped and cheered?

Everyone.

. . . . .

After my triumph during the spelling bee, I figured it was safe to go to the lunchroom. Over the past twenty-four hours, everyone had been hearing I was innocent, and that's all that mattered. I got a tray of tater tot hot dish and sat next to Bao. "Epic finish, Charlotte." Bao smiled at me *and* made eye contact. Emma said, "What a weird week."

My mood crashed when Emma said, "If I'd have known Julia's dad was in town, I would've guessed right away that it was him. Poor Julia. It's not her fault."

I knew I'd cleared Julia's dad. Julia knew I'd cleared her dad. But I hadn't told Mr. Crenski yet. I looked around the cafeteria and didn't see Julia anywhere. "Where is Julia?"

"I don't know," Emma said. "She's probably avoiding

everyone because of her dad. When he went to jail for the robbery, it was pretty rough. People were mean to her, especially the boys."

Bao rolled her eyes. "Boys are the worst."

"Everyone has old information, and it's wrong," I said. "It wasn't Julia's father. It was Bad Chad."

At the same time Emma and Bao said, "Seriously?" Katie Turner and Lanie Erickson leaned toward us and said, "Bad Chad?"

I had to take a deep breath to get the words out. "I saw him myself."

"I'm not surprised," Emma said. "He's a loser."

"Why didn't the police talk to him first?" Katie asked. "They should've guessed he was the one. Everyone knows he's trouble."

"Did Julia go home?" Emma wondered.

"No," I said. "I know where to find her."

I put my lunch tray on the counter and walked down the hall to the bathroom. Sure enough, I spotted Julia's sneakers in the bathroom's last stall.

"Julia?"

She didn't answer.

"Julia, I know it's you."

She opened the door. She was wiping tears with a wad of toilet paper. "I just didn't want to deal with it again."

"I told everyone about Bad Chad. You don't have to hide."

"Did you talk to the principal this morning?"

"No. Not yet."

She frowned. "The news needs to come from him. That's when people will really believe it." My stomach clenched because she was right, and I couldn't avoid Mr. Crenski much longer. "Why are you waiting? Go now."

"Maybe after school. I don't want to be late for class. Mrs. Lester is a monster."

"Mr. Crenski will give us passes."

"Us?"

Julia blew her nose and flushed the paper. "I'm going with you, but let's wait in a stall until the bell rings. I don't want to see people in the hall. Not yet. Not until it's officially over."

We crammed into the stall together.

"You were wrong, Charlotte," Julia said.

"I know. Your dad didn't do it."

"That's not what I mean. You were wrong about Gloria and Teresa. I saw Gloria yesterday, and I told her that you overheard them saying our work wasn't good and they couldn't pay me."

You know that feeling right before you realize you made a mistake? The feeling that hits before the words?

WHAM! I felt punched in the stomach. Then Julia spoke.

"They got a bill for fixing the roof, and the bill was a lot more than the guy told them it was going to be. They don't have the money in the budget for it, so they're hoping he'll waive the extra charges and consider it a donation. She said it's his fault because he gave them a bad estimate. And guess what? It's still leaking. His work is bad quality. Not ours. His."

I'd assumed the worst.

Again.

A big, fat, epic mistake.

I slapped my hands over my face. "I screwed up. Big time."

Julia grabbed my arm. "You can deal with that later. We've got to see Mr. Crenski. Come on."

I let Julia lead me all the way to Mr. Crenski's office. With each step, I lost my confidence about the Bad Chad story. My hands shook. My throat tightened. Words tumbled in my brain.

When we sat in Mr. Crenski's office, Julia didn't wait for him to ask why we'd come. She blurted out the words. "Charlotte has important information about the museum."

Mr. Crenski's eyebrows arched. "Again?"

I wished Julia could talk for me. My mouth wasn't cooperating.

"I'm waiting," Mr. Crenski said.

How was I going to get through this?

Finally I said, "You can tell him, Julia, if you want."

"I need to hear from you."

I pressed my hands against the chair to keep them from shaking. I told myself I had to do this for Julia. I shouldn't have blamed her dad. I had to fix it.

"I made a mistake that resulted in the wrong conclusion.

246

Remember how I told you that I looked out the window and saw a guy with spray paint?"

"I remember. In fact, I can't forget."

"Well, I assumed it was Julia's dad, but I've never actually seen Julia's dad. Sometimes I assume the wrong thing, the worst thing, and I want to stop doing that. Turns out Julia's dad is short and chubby, and the guy I saw was tall . . . tall and thin . . . and maybe—"

"Bad Chad!" Julia said. "She saw Bad Chad."

I nodded. "Bad Chad is this teenager who hangs out in the park."

"Chad Larson. I'm aware." He leaned forward. "What makes you think it was Chad Larson?"

"Julia told me her dad wasn't tall."

"There are lots of tall teenagers and men in Walnut Grove. Why do you think it was Chad Larson?"

Did he have to ask me that? Couldn't he just write down the name and send us to class? I wished Mrs. Lester would burst through the door and call Mr. Crenski a lazy ninnyhammer for the lack of spelling tests in this school.

"Charlotte?"

"Once she said that, I sort of remembered more about how he really looked." I sputtered. "And he really looked like Bad Chad."

"Charlotte, your memory of events has had quite the evolution. Are you certain?"

"One hundred percent." Julia spoke for me. "She told me she was one hundred percent sure."

Mr. Crenski stared at me for a moment. Then he said, "I want Charlotte to tell me herself. Are you certain?"

He was setting me up. I could tell by looking in his eyes. I was a terrible liar. He knew if I kept talking I'd miss something along the way. But I was in too deep. I gulped. "Yes. Certain. I am certain and sure."

"Why wouldn't she be?" Julia asked.

"I talked to the police yesterday and told them about Charlotte's most recent explanation involving your father. They made an interesting point, which still applies. Because Chad Larson is sixteen years old, almost a full-grown man. There were small footprints in the snow around the building. I'm pretty sure Chad Larson doesn't wear size five boots."

The boots!

I'd completely forgotten about the boots.

It was too much. Tears were dripping off my chin before I even realized I was crying.

Julia's face turned white. "What? Why are you crying?"

"Because I didn't see anyone or anything!" The words poured out. "I slept all night. I just want everyone to know it wasn't me."

Mr. Crenski shook his head. He started to speak, but I didn't hear a word. I ran down the stairs. I didn't stop at my locker for my boots or coat. I ran out the building, down the street, past the park, through our neighborhood. I ran to that stupid basement, a place that was home only because my mother was there.

TWENTY-FIVE

But Mom wasn't home. She was gone. Freddy had our cell phone in his locker, so I couldn't call or text her. If she'd gone to the Asian grocery, she'd be back in a few minutes, but if she'd gone shopping in Marshall, it could be hours.

I flopped onto the bed, but I couldn't nap. Even though my eyes were closed, it felt like they were open. I tried reading *Harry Potter*, but the words blurred together. I went to the closet to get the Jack bag, but it was gone. Rose had told me she was sleeping with it. I shifted the blankets on her bed until I found it. I wrapped my arms around the bag like it was the living Jack. I squeezed him and tried to remember everything about him—his coarse fur, his nose against my cheek, his high-pitched whine. I would've given anything to smell his rotten breath again.

I heard footsteps and voices. Mom and someone else.

I went to the bedroom door and saw Mom in the kitchen, unpacking groceries and laughing with Shorty.

"Mom!"

Both Mom and Shorty jumped.

"Charlotte? What's going on? Why are you home?" Her lips were covered with dark pink lipstick, and she'd curled her hair.

"Why is he here?"

"I'm making lunch for us." She put her hand on my forehead. "Are you sick?"

I didn't even care that Shorty could hear me. I couldn't keep the lies inside me a second longer. "I had the worst day ever. I told Principal Crenski that Julia's dad vandalized the museum. Then I said Bad Chad did it. I don't actually know who did it. I lied about everything except for the part about it not being me."

Mom froze. She stood there, just holding a gallon of milk and staring at me.

"I'm sorry," I whispered.

Shorty took the milk and gave her a nudge.

Finally she blinked. "I don't know what to say."

"I don't either. I didn't want to lie. I just want people to believe me." I started to cry.

"I know." Mom hugged me tight. "Lying is not okay, but you did it out of fear, not malice. That's an important distinction."

"Now they'll never believe me. I'm like the boy who

cried wolf, because once you lie everyone thinks you're a liar."

"You made a bad choice. That doesn't make you a bad person."

Shorty said, "I should leave so you can talk. You still want to go to Minneapolis later?"

"You're going to Minneapolis?"

"Freddy's hearing aid is ready," Mom said. "We have to bring Freddy to test it and get the settings right. The problem is the car's check-engine light came on. I can't take it out of town until it's fixed. Shorty offered to drive us."

That happened with every car we owned. It meant a repair Mom couldn't afford. With Freddy's expensive hearing aid and the car problems, I knew Mom would soon say words that led to packing: *A problem is an opportunity to start again.* This time, though, I had a few friends and even a nickname. I was a spelling bee champion and the museum's idea person. But I was also a "vandal" and "liar."

"Are we going to Minneapolis after school?"

Shorty shook his head. "Sorry, Charlotte, but I've got a pickup without a back seat. I can only take two people."

Mom sighed. "The plan is to pick Freddy up at school on our way out of town, get to the store before they close, and turn around and drive right back. But maybe we should do it tomorrow. I'm not sure I can leave Charlotte like this." She looked at Shorty.

"If we wait until tomorrow," he said, "we'll get caught in

the snow that's coming. Then I don't have help at the station for a few days."

Mom nodded. "And Freddy needs his hearing aid . . ." She squeezed my hand. "I really don't want to leave you, though."

I was done crying, but my breath came in deep and ragged. "I'll be fine. Rose will be home soon."

Mom's phone rang. She answered it, listened for a few seconds, and said, "Hold on." She pressed the phone against her stomach so the caller couldn't hear. "It's Mr. Crenski. I'm going to take it in my bedroom."

"Please don't make me go back to school today."

"I'll tell him you're spending the rest of the day at home. And I'll tell him we're going to pick Freddy up now. Why wait until after school? The sooner we get going, the sooner we can get back."

"Ask him about Mrs. Newman."

"What?"

"Ask him when she's coming back. Please."

She shook her head. "One thing at a time, Charlotte."

Mom went to her bedroom, and I sat at the table. Shorty got a glass from the cupboard, filled it with milk, and brought it to me. He knew exactly which cabinet held our glasses. Obviously he'd been spending time here while we were at school.

I said, "You hear everything at the gas station. What's going to happen to Mrs. Newman?"

He shrugged. "I don't think I've got the facts yet. Some

people say she's getting fired. One guy told me she quit and took a teaching job in Marshall. But other folks are saying she's suspended for two weeks and will be back."

"Suspended? Is that sort of like detention for teachers?"

"I guess so."

"It's not fair. She was only trying to help me. It's my fault."

He pulled off his Twins baseball cap and scratched his head. A tuft of blond hair stood straight up. "She made a choice. She could've kept her nose out of it, but she defended a kid. And defending a kid is a pretty good choice, if you ask me." He sighed. "But nobody ever asks me."

"It's not fair."

"Life isn't fair, and Angie Newman knows that."

It was weird to hear that Mrs. Newman had a first name like a real person. "Does she have kids?"

"Yup." He smiled. "Two at home and twenty-four at school."

. . . . .

When Rose came home, I told her about the trip to Minneapolis while I made an early dinner for us—grilled cheese and popcorn.

"It's already snowing," she said.

"A little or a lot?"

"I'm not hungry. You don't have to cook for me."

I turned on the radio and found the station that played

polka music. I knew the announcers there gave weather reports every hour. "You look like you have fever 'n' ague."

Rose shrugged. "I'm just not hungry."

I asked again, "Is it snowing a little or a lot?"

"A little, but it's windy."

The grilled cheese sandwiches were brown on both sides. I flipped the sandwiches onto plates and got the popcorn bag from the microwave. "At least take a few bites."

The chirpy polka faded and the announcer said, "Folks, get ready to shovel. The weather system is shifting west. Our friends to the east can rest easy, but we'll have at least eight inches on the ground by morning. Temperatures will drop to five degrees, but it'll feel like minus twenty with the wind chill. Expect gusts of wind up to thirty miles an hour. We'll report school closings as they come in."

I turned off the radio. "I bet there's no school tomorrow. But what if Mom can't make it home?"

Rose shrugged. I sent Mom a text about the weather and she replied right away. *No snow here. You sure?* So I took the phone outside. Under the streetlight you could see snow falling against the dark sky. I snapped a picture and texted it to her with a note. *See?*

When I got downstairs, Rose was picking the crust off her grilled cheese. "What'd Mom say?"

Just then Mom texted. *I don't want you home alone tonight. Shorty says he has four-wheel drive and knows how to manage these roads. We'll take it slow. Don't wait up.*

"They're coming home, but it'll be late." I flopped onto the couch. "I'm so tired."

"But you had a good day, right?"

"Hah!" I snorted. "I had the worst day of my life."

She sat on the edge of the recliner and bit her lip. "But they're not blaming you anymore, right?"

"Where'd you get that idea?"

"In gym Olivia said everyone knew it was Julia's dad. Then Frankie Simon told me it was Bad Chad. Either way, you're off the hook."

Her perky voice annoyed me. I crossed my arms. "Your friends are behind. Mr. Crenski and the police still think it's me."

"I don't get it. I thought it was over."

"It's not over. Not even close. Mrs. Newman is probably going to get fired, and Julia is never going to speak to me again, and I'll probably get arrested."

"You're focusing on the negative."

"Where's the rainbow, Rose?" I watched her struggle to find sunny words. I felt tears coming again. My voice cracked. "What if they put me in jail?"

Rose shook her head. "I'll never let that happen. I swear. I'll tell them it was me."

"Don't be stupid. Why would you even say that?"

She stared at her feet, arms stiff, hands rolled into fists. With a deep breath, she said, "Because it was me."

Her words seemed to float in the air before they

actually registered in my brain. I wondered if that's how Freddy's hearing aids worked. Was there a delay? Did they grab words hanging in the air and send them to the brain?

Finally I said, "What?"

Her eyes were big and scared. She clenched her fists and stammered in a voice so hoarse it was almost like she had laryngitis, "I don't know what got into me. I just exploded. It's like I wasn't in my body."

I couldn't believe what I was hearing, so I said it again. "What?"

"It's been the worst year ever. Dad and his stupid wife and his stupid twins."

"Stupid twins? I don't get it."

She wiped tears on her sleeves. The words tumbled out faster. "That night it all happened he forgot we were supposed to talk online. I woke up at midnight and there was a text from him. They're having twins." She spit out the words. "More stupid twins!"

"So you spray painted the museum? I don't believe you." The utter surprise held back my anger. "You love Laura Ingalls."

"Laura Ingalls doesn't love us! She won't connect with Mom. Laura's energy is angry because Mom is writing about Mars instead of the prairie. If that book doesn't start writing itself, we'll have to leave. And when we leave, Freddy will lose all those friends, and he'll hog you all to himself. Just like before. I'll be an only child all over again, only this time Dad won't want me, either."

I waited for the anger. It didn't come—just disbelief. For a moment, I convinced myself I'd taken a nap and just woke up. Shorty was never here. Mom never left for Minneapolis. I never made grilled cheese. This conversation never happened. In a few seconds it'd be the four of us having dinner followed by a night of homework.

"I hate everything!" she shouted. "Everything! Everyone. I hate you!"

"Me? You get me into trouble and *you* hate *me*?"

"All you care about is Freddy."

Finally the anger bubbled in my stomach and blew like a volcano. "Rose Martha Mendoza! You're worse than Bad Chad!"

She sniffled and said, "I didn't plan it. I was just going to walk around because I was so mad about Dad and what you said about Freddy."

"I don't remember saying a single word about Freddy."

"You wanted to ask him what he thought."

"So?"

"Basically you meant you want everything to be the way it was. You know, when it was just the two of you. Admit it. I'm not wrong. Am I wrong?"

"Even if you're right—and I'm not saying you're right—what difference does it make?" I yelled. "You don't get to be a thug because you think your sister likes your brother better!"

She lifted her head and blinked back tears.

"So I am right." Rose crossed her arms. I should've

257

corrected her, but I didn't. I was too angry. "Well, then, on my way out, I saw the spray paint on the shelf and grabbed it to write in the snow. That's all. But the more I walked, the madder I got. I was thinking about the museum ladies taking the money and saying things about Mom, and Laura's bad energy, and—"

"I don't want to hear your lame excuses. We are calling the police right now!"

"Don't!" she said. "Don't call yet. They might go after Bad Chad. Wait. Just wait awhile."

"Wait? Are you kidding? When I go to school, everyone is going to be talking about me and blaming me!"

"But as far as they know, it could be Bad Chad!"

"Are you not getting this? Mr. Crenski knows I didn't see Bad Chad."

Rose gulped. "But maybe—"

"You're an idiot!" I shouted. "Get out of here! I hate you!"

She grabbed her coat and ran up the stairs. I yelled, "I hope you get lost in a blizzard."

The door slammed so hard the windows rattled.

· CHAPTER ·

TWENTY-SIX

Ten minutes later, I was still pacing from the bottom of the stairs in the kitchen to our bedroom. Back and forth, back and forth, trying to decide what to do. Should I call Mom? Mia? The police? After lying about Julia's dad and Bad Chad, the police would have no reason to believe me when I said I didn't do it. Nope, not me. It was my *sister*.

I wasn't even sure I wanted them to believe me, because that meant Rose was in trouble. In between flashes of anger, I felt sorry for Rose. Freddy and my Twin Superpowers made her an outsider, but I had never realized it hurt her. She was Mom's shadow, so it evened out.

Right?

Instead of dialing 911, I texted Julia. *Can you talk?*

Her response was immediate. *Leave me alone!!!!!!*

I know what really happened. For real this time.
I'M TURNING MY PHONE OFF!

Great. I was probably the only person who'd ever made Julia Ramos mad enough to type in all caps. I decided to wait for Mom to come home and let her figure it out. I needed to get Rose inside. She was probably pouting in the garage. Then I remembered I'd left my winter gear at school. As I wrapped a blanket around me, our phone buzzed. I grabbed it, hoping it was Julia, but it was Mom. *On our way. Slow going.* I thought about what to say. Finally I just typed, *OK*. No reason to tell her everything until she showed up.

But Rose wasn't in the garage. When I opened the door to the backyard, the wind nearly knocked me over. Ice pellets scratched my face. Between the darkness and snow, I could barely see the trees at the edge of the lawn. There was no sign of Rose. I forced the door shut against the wind and went to the front of the garage and opened the door to the driveway. If Rose had left prints in the snow, they would've been covered by the wind. I stepped outside and yelled Rose's name. In my sneakers, I trudged through the snow and looked in Mom's car, which was parked on the street. No Rose. I yelled her name again, but the howling wind seemed to absorb my voice. The cold cut through to my bones.

If she wasn't outside, where was she?

I had one more place to check—Mia's minivan, which

was in the garage. It'd be just like Rose to hide in the back seat.

But she wasn't there, either.

She'd left with her coat. No boots, no hat, no mittens. There's no way she would've rushed down the street in a storm. No way.

Except that she was scared.

And confused.

And mad.

Obviously she'd turn around. She'd be back in a couple minutes. I leaned against the van and waited, shivering the whole time. I thought about pioneers who died in blizzards because they got lost going from their barns to their houses.

Then I realized she probably hadn't gone anywhere at all. She'd gone upstairs to see Mia. I knocked on the door, and Miguel answered.

"Did Rose come up here?"

"No. What's going on?"

My words flew out. "Rose is gone. I think she's outside in the storm, and I don't know what to do."

Mia and Julia appeared next to Miguel. "What's wrong, honey?" Mia asked.

"Rose ran away! She's in the storm. She told me she vandalized the museum and we—"

Mia's eyes widened. "Rose? Rose vandalized the museum?"

"She told me and we got in a huge fight and she took

off and I didn't know the storm was this bad and I can't find her."

Miguel was already putting on his jacket. "Let's go. Julia, wait here in case Rose comes back. Charlotte can come with us."

"Where's your jacket?" Mia asked.

"I left it at school."

"She can wear mine." Julia brought me her jacket, hat, and mittens. "Grandpa, how can you drive in this?"

Miguel said, "We won't leave town. We'll just go up and down the streets. We'll cover more ground than walking. There's no way she went far. She's probably at the park."

She was probably at the park.

She was definitely at the park.

Right?

. . . . .

The van crept down the street with windshield wipers on full speed, which was useless. The wind whipped the snow into a swirling cloud. Miguel turned the headlights on the bright setting, which also was useless. Every few feet he'd stop the van and look for a house or tree or street sign—anything to indicate how far we'd come. Mia rolled down the window and yelled Rose's name. Snow pelted her face, and the howling wind drowned out her voice.

"Are we at the intersection with the park?" Miguel asked.

"I can't tell," Mia answered.

I said, "I'm going to text my mother."

Mia turned around. "Don't. She'll panic, and there's nothing she can do. She's stuck in Minneapolis."

"She's coming back."

"Don't be silly," Mia said. "She's not driving in this."

"Yes, she is. But I'm guessing she shouldn't be, right?" I leaned back in the seat and groaned. "Great. Both my sister and my mom could die in a blizzard."

"She rode with Shorty, didn't she?" Miguel asked. "Personally, I wouldn't drive in it. But Shorty is one of those stubborn guys who's been driving through prairie winters his whole life. He's got a four-wheel-drive pickup truck. They'll make it. They might sit on the side of the road until morning, but they'll make it." Miguel stopped the van. "That's the park."

Again Mia yelled out the window for Rose.

I said, "I'll go look."

"No," Miguel said. "It's too dangerous."

"I'll come right back if I don't see her."

"You might lose sight of the van. We don't need two lost kids. People die in this weather."

"Silencio!" Mia shushed him in Spanish as if I couldn't understand she was telling him to be quiet and not scare me. Too late. I was terrified.

"What if she slips on the ice and hits her head and passes out? What if she wanders on the highway and the plow hits her?"

"That's not going to happen." Mia stretched into the back seat and patted my leg like her magic hand could put me in a calm trance.

Miguel said, "We've done all we can do. We need to call the police."

The grilled cheese sandwich churned in my stomach and threatened to come back up. "Can the police cars get through?"

"They'll need trucks." Slowly he turned the van around. "Or the county could send the plow. We'll figure it out."

"We sure will," Mia said.

"Yes," Miguel said. "We will."

Mia called the police and reported that Rose was lost somewhere in town while Miguel assured me it was going to be fine, just fine, nothing to worry about at all, nope, it was all going to end with Rose at one of the neighbor's houses drinking hot chocolate and eating cookies and calling us, and we were going to feel silly calling 911 for no reason whatsoever.

By the time Mia finished describing Rose's winter gear to the police officer, we were back in the garage. Inside the house, Mia made us hot chocolate, and I told them everything about my argument with Rose, including her confession. They stared at me in disbelief. Nobody believed Rose would do such a thing. Then I burst into tears and stammered, "I yelled at her. I said I hoped she'd get lost in a blizzard."

"You didn't mean it," Julia said. "Besides, Pa Ingalls got

lost in blizzards a couple of times every year. He was always lost in a blizzard. He'd dig a snow cave."

"Rose doesn't know how to dig a snow cave."

"Rose watched YouTube videos on how to churn butter. She knows all about snow caves. I'm positive." Julia's perky voice reminded me of Rose the rainbow-finder. She was more reassuring than Mia, who kept patting me on the back.

Miguel said, "She's not wandering around the prairie. She's in town somewhere. She's bound to end up at someone's house. We'll get a phone call any minute from a neighbor or the police."

"Someone will call." Mia gave each of us a cookie. "Any minute."

Minutes passed.

An hour passed.

The phone didn't ring.

TWENTY-SEVEN

Shortly after midnight, the wind's howl turned to a whimper. Julia slept in the recliner, but Mia, Miguel, and I sat on the couch and stared at the clock. Miguel parted the drapes and looked outside. "The snow has mostly stopped. I think I'll drive around the park again."

"Can you get through the snow?" Mia asked.

"If we get rid of the snow that's blown against the garage, I think I can get to the street. If I get stuck, I'll just walk back and wait for the plow."

"I'll help shovel," I said.

Julia's eyes popped open. "Is the storm over?"

"We're going to clear out the driveway and drive to the park," I said.

"I'll help, too."

This time I bundled up in Mia's gear. Under the street-lights, the three of us made quick work of clearing the driveway. I'd helped Miguel with the sidewalk and drive-way before. Shoveling was an odd chore. No matter how cold it was, after a few minutes of lifting and dumping snow, you'd sweat like crazy. Your face would ache from the cold, but your back would be sticky from sweat.

When we had half of the driveway clear, Miguel said, "Let's give it a try. Hopefully I won't get stuck in the street."

Julia and I shoveled the sidewalk as he backed out and drove down the street. The van moved ten feet; then the tires spun and spit snow. The van fishtailed and came to a stop. Miguel shifted the van from forward to reverse and back again, but he was stuck. Miguel, Julia, and I shov-eled a path behind the van to the driveway. Then Miguel backed up, pulled into the driveway, and parked in the garage.

"I'll take a little walk," he said. "You girls go inside and get warm."

Inside Mia made another round of hot chocolate and opened a can of chicken noodle soup. "The police called. No news yet. And your mom texted. They're at a gas sta-tion waiting for a plow to go through. I didn't say anything about Rose. No reason to make her panic. She'd force Shorty to venture out ahead of the plow, and they'd end up in a ditch."

"Maybe you should tell her."

"Trust me. I'm a mother."

Julia stirred marshmallows into cups of hot chocolate and handed a cup to me. "Let's think like Rose. If you were Rose, and you ran off because you were scared and mad, where would you go?"

"Rose never gets scared and mad."

"I bet she went to the museum. Maybe she broke into the sod house and hunkered down there. It'd be easy to get into it."

"Maybe," I said. "Should we look?"

"You're both staying here. When Miguel gets back, I'll talk to him about it."

I sipped the hot chocolate and tried to think of anything except Rose. My brain jumped from subject to subject, but Rose stayed in the mix. Mrs. Newman, Mrs. Lester, Rose. Jack, Freddy, Rose. Bao, Emma, Rose. Rose and Rose and Rose.

Julia said, "She's going to be okay."

"She will," Mia said. "I've been praying all night. Jesus protects children."

I nodded and thought of the spelling bee and how Laura's energy delivered *transcontinental* to me. I silently asked Laura for help—Laura because she survived one of the worst winters on record, Laura because she loved her sisters, and Laura because she knew Rose's heart was gold, even if she'd done a bad thing.

Would Laura forgive Rose?

My heart said yes.

Mia said, "The police officer said they put an announcement on the radio. Someone will find her."

Her news didn't make me feel better.

Who's listening to the radio at two a.m.?

Nobody.

Except, it turned out, for one person.

Rose. Rose was listening to the radio at two a.m.

. . . . .

When Mia's cell phone rang at 2:15 in the morning, she looked stunned. "It's your mom."

"Put her on speaker," I said.

"Hello," Mia said. "I've got you on speaker."

"Is Charlotte with you?"

"I'm here, Mom."

Mom sighed with relief. "Rose just called me. She's safe."

Mia and Julia hugged each other.

"Where is she?" I asked.

"She said you two got in a fight, and she ran outside and got disoriented in the snow. She ended up at Shorty's station. She went inside, but the clerk was in the back room. She was afraid, I guess, so she hid in the bathroom. I don't know why she didn't find the clerk and tell him she needed help."

I knew why—she didn't want to have to explain what she was running from. Apparently Rose hadn't told Mom the whole story.

"Is she still there?" Mia asked.

Mom cleared her throat. "The clerk closed early and made it home. When he left, Rose got some food and water and sat in Shorty's office listening to the radio. When she heard the alert, she knew she needed to call."

Mia put her hand on her heart. "Thank the Lord."

"Charlotte, why were you fighting with Rose? And why didn't you call me?"

"It's complicated," I said.

"Charlotte can explain when you get home," Mia said. "Complicated doesn't begin to describe it. Just be safe. I'll see if the county can get the plow here right away. We'll get her home."

"Thank you, Mia." Mom sounded really tired. "Charlotte, sounds like we have a lot to talk about. Get some sleep, okay?"

"Okay."

The call ended. I didn't even care if Mom was mad at me. She'd get the real story soon enough. Rose was safe, and that's all that mattered.

While Miguel went to get Rose, Mia shuffled Julia and me into Julia's bedroom and told us to get some sleep. I was wide-awake, though. We'd been going full speed all night, and the energy didn't stop pumping just because the lights were out. I needed Julia to understand what had happened.

"Julia, I just found out the truth today. I wasn't hiding it from you to protect Rose."

"I know."

"I made up the stuff about your dad and Bad Chad because—"

"Just stop, okay? I'm glad Rose is okay, but I don't forgive you for bringing my dad into it and making me feel bad. Not just bad, Charlotte. Awful."

My heart nearly melted. This was worse than Molly Smith. Way worse. I'd lost Molly because Mom had made us move. I had nobody to blame for losing Julia except myself.

"Can we talk about it?"

"I'm tired," she said. "I just want to sleep."

I whispered, "Okay."

Julia's breathing slowed, and in a few minutes I could tell she was sleeping. But I couldn't close my eyes. Mia opened the door and peeked inside. She whispered, "Still awake?"

"Yes."

"The radio says there's no school tomorrow. You can sleep late."

"Is Rose back?"

"She's on the couch, but she's already out cold. Your mom says they're behind a plow now. Probably an hour away."

"Did you tell her about Rose and the museum?"

Mia sighed. "I gave her the short version. She asked what set everything off, so I told her."

"Okay. Good."

Mia closed the door. I waited until the hall lights snapped off. Then I got up and went to the living room. Rose was wrapped in a blanket on the couch. Her long hair curled around her chin, and her cheeks were chapped from the cold. First I wanted to hug her. Then I wanted to take a pillow and hit her with it. Then I wanted to hug her again. How was it possible to be happy and relieved to see her but also feel angry? Worse than angry—furious. It was like sweating in the cold. Nothing in Walnut Grove made sense.

Instead of going back to Julia's room, I settled into the recliner near Rose.

No school tomorrow? Good.

But sleep late?

Hah. I'd be lucky if I slept at all.

TWENTY-EIGHT

After lunch the next day, after we'd all had plenty of rest, Mom set up her essential oil diffuser and put a drop of lavender oil in it. "This will help us relax and stay focused while we talk about what happened," she said. Within minutes, the basement smelled wonderful. Rose told Mom everything—about feeling like an only child her whole life, about Rey and his new wife and their twins, about the museum ladies saying mean things about Mom and trash-talking my project, about Laura abandoning Mom and her writing. At that point, Mom dabbed essential oil on her wrists.

Then Rose told her something she hadn't told me. "I read Charlotte's school assignment about the Trail of Tears. The article was about how settling the West destroyed the Indians. They literally had to walk hundreds of miles so the pioneers could have their land. And they got sick and there wasn't enough food and the weather was terrible, but the government didn't care and the pioneers didn't care. The Indians had to keep marching, and tons of them died. Tons!"

At that point, Mom dabbed the oil behind her ears.

Rose said, "We have museums all over the United States bragging about how great we are because we built a new country. We have books and movies and songs. But our stories are wrong." Her shoulders slumped. "Can I try some of that oil?"

I put a drop on my finger and rubbed it on Rose's wrist. Freddy said, "I know what you mean, but I'm glad we're here. I'm glad there are fifty states and roads and the Internet and that I get to live in this country."

"If you're glad, then you don't know what I mean," Rose said.

Freddy crossed his arms. "How does spray-painting a building make it better? That's just dumb, Rose."

"I'm not dumb. You're dumb!"

"I didn't say *you* are dumb. I said *what you did* is dumb."

"Let's not use the word *dumb*," Mom said. "It's not a productive word."

"Speaking of dumb, what's with L-A-R-A?" I asked.

"I started to panic about getting caught, but it was too late. I'd sprayed the building. At the last second, I figured if I misspelled Laura they'd think it was someone who didn't know much about her."

"So you decided to spray-paint Laura's building because the government was terrible to the Indians?" Freddy said. "Am I the only one who thinks that's ridiculous?"

"No. I think it's ridiculous," I said.

"Let her finish," Mom said. "Go on, Rose."

Rose frowned. "Here's something I bet you didn't know. In the first version of *Little House on the Prairie*, which came out almost one hundred years ago, Laura described the prairie like this: 'There the wild animals wandered and fed as though they were in a pasture that stretched much farther than a man could see, and there were no people. Only Indians lived there.' I memorized it."

Freddy thought for a minute. "So? What's your point?"

"She said no people. Only Indians. She basically said Indians aren't people."

Slowly Freddy's face registered her point. Mom said, "I don't remember that. I've read that book a dozen times."

"Someone wrote to the publisher, and they changed the word *people* to *settlers* for the next printing. Laura felt terrible about it. She didn't mean it the way it came out. Still, it bugs me. I can't stop thinking about it. That's why I quit reading the biography."

"I had no idea," Mom said. "How did I not know this?"

"That's the way people were back then," Freddy said. "It's not right to blame people now for what happened one hundred years ago. Laura Ingalls didn't force the Indians to move. The museum ladies didn't force them to move, either. Do you want us to demolish all our cities and make it buffalo land again?"

"That's not the point!" Rose yelled. "You got me all side-tracked."

"We don't yell in this family," Mom said. "Speak calmly or go to your room until you can."

"Fine. I won't yell." Rose took a deep breath. "I wasn't mad at Laura. Laura's building just happened to be there, and all that information about Laura and the Trail of Tears just happened to be fresh in my head." Rose stewed for a few seconds and then spit out the words, "I was mad at *her*." She pointed at me.

"Me?"

"All you wanted that night was Freddy. You wanted everything to be the way it used to be. Just the two of you together all the time."

"That's not true." I said it without force because, in a way, it was true.

"I'm nothing to you. I'm nobody. I'm just the ghost sister."

"Now that is *definitely* not true. You're a great sister. The best!"

"It's always been you two against me. This year he dumped you. And I've been there for you. Me! Still you like him better, even though he's a big jerk."

Mom gasped.

Freddy frowned and stared at his feet.

I didn't know what to say. I wished with every cell in my body that Bad Chad was the villain. If Rose was the villain, and Bad Chad was Innocent Chad, then I didn't understand the world at all. I'd always thought I had people figured out, but I'd made a lot of mistakes in Walnut Grove. Julia wasn't fake-nice. She was nice-nice. Mrs. Newman wasn't mean. She was brave. And Bao was more than Purple Glasses Girl. She was a friend.

"I don't know what to say about any of this." Mom sighed. "I'm rarely at a loss for words. Rose, you have to tell the police what you did."

"I know."

"And you have to figure out a way to make it right with Charlotte. Obviously I'm upset about what you did, but I'm devastated that you'd stand by and let Charlotte suffer."

"I know!" Rose stood up and paced. "I could hardly stand it. You have to believe me. It was eating me up. I wasn't going to let Charlotte get in trouble. I swear I planned to admit it. I was waiting for the universe to send me courage."

"That's totally lame." My temper was rising again, but it cooled as soon as I saw the look on Mom's face.

Mom's hands shook and her voice cracked. "Our family is broken."

I'd never heard Mom sound like that. I put my arm around her. "We're not broken." I tried to think of something that would make her feel better. "We're . . . healing. You can't have . . . um, joy . . . if you don't sometimes have pain."

Freddy got a roll of toilet paper and gave a wad to Mom. She said, "I thought we were a close family."

"We are!" I said. "And now we'll be even closer."

"I'm sorry I broke us," Rose whispered.

Mom wiped her eyes and blew her nose. "You didn't break us. Charlotte's right. We'll come through this even stronger than before. You make this family complete, Rose. I love you. I'm proud of your beautiful heart."

Freddy sighed. "A guy can only take so much of this stuff. I need a time-out." Freddy tossed me the roll of toilet paper and went into his bedroom.

Mom and Rose snuggled on the couch, and Mom patted the seat next to her. But I said, "I'll be back in a few minutes."

I followed Freddy to his room where he was reading text messages. I said, "Freddy, will you close the door?"

"Why?"

"Because if one of us has to get shocked, it should be you."

He frowned but didn't argue. When he touched the doorknob, I literally heard the zap. He rubbed his hand, sat on the bed, and glared at me. "What?"

The phone chirped, and I grabbed it from his hand before he could read the message. I wanted to throw it, but Mom couldn't afford a new hearing aid, a car repair, and a new phone. I pushed aside the stack of folded T-shirts on his dresser to make room for the phone. The shirts fell to the floor, which was already covered with dirty clothes, books, folders, and granola-bar wrappers. His room smelled like sweaty socks and sour milk. I didn't miss this part of sharing a room with Freddy. Rose made her bed every morning and mine, too, if I forgot. She organized her socks by color, and her books were always stacked alphabetically by the author's last name. Rose was the anti-Freddy.

"Those shirts are clean. Thanks for nothing." He put the shirts back on the dresser in a heap, took the phone, and flopped onto his bed. "You've been acting like this for months. I'm sick of it."

"You're sick of it? That's hilarious. Because I am completely and totally sick of Red Fred. And you know what else, Red Fred? Part of what happened here is *your* fault."

"Rose and the museum? That's not my fault."

"I'll just say what everybody is thinking." I tried to hold my voice steady. "You abandoned Rose."

"Did not!"

"Yes, Freddy, you did."

He rolled his eyes. "Rose and I are the same as we've always been. Nothing's changed."

"You abandoned Rose. You made her feel alone."

"Oh yeah?" He stood up and put his hands on his hips. "Evidence?"

"You stopped eating lunch with her! You stopped talking to her!" I got nearly nose-to-nose with him. I closed my eyes and took a deep breath. *Be brave.*

281

I opened my eyes and blurted out the words. "Observation: this isn't about Rose. Clearly I'm talking about *me*. It's always been you and me against the world. Until now. You abandoned *me*!"

Freddy backed up until he hit the bed. Then he sat down and slumped his shoulders.

"You keep acting like I pushed you out of everything. And that's not true. I tried to pull you in, but you wouldn't come."

"What happened? How'd you turn into this social guy in the one week I was sick?"

Freddy shrugged. "I've never been on my own before. Ever! I was forced to actually think for myself and talk for myself. You know, that first day, when I left for school, I'd never been so scared. I thought about skipping school and hiding somewhere all day. But then—"

"I know, I know. You told a joke, and everyone laughed. So good-bye, Charlotte."

"I handled it by myself, and it went fine. It went great. And those guys turned out to be cool, and now I have actual friends."

"Actual friends? I'm your sister and an actual friend all rolled into one. Twin Superpowers!"

"A guy can only take so much lavender oil and Laura Ingalls and positive affirmations and girl stuff . . ." He threw his hands in the air. "Now I have some actual *guy* friends. Why is that so hard to understand?"

I never thought about Freddy struggling with being

the only boy in our family. Even if he had a point, he was setting himself up for huge disappointment. "Well, we're leaving. Maybe not this week or this month, but we will leave."

He nodded. "But now I know I can do it. I can make friends."

"You think you're going to be a rock star in a big-city school?"

"I don't care about being Mr. Popular. I care about having two or three friends. Or just one friend. Admit it: you like Bao and Emma and Julia."

"That doesn't change the fact that you abandoned me."

He picked up the phone. "I want to show you something." He scanned through some text messages and handed the phone to me.

Noah: WTH? Is gazelle in trouble?

Freddy: No way. She would never ever ever do that. I swear.

Between him and Katie:

Katie: If your sister did it, that's awful.

Freddy: She didn't. Innocent until proven guilty.

Katie: Well it was awful. Can't blame people for being mad.

Freddy: If I'm wrong, and she did it, be mad at both of us. But SHE DIDN'T.

Between him and Ethan:

Freddy: Someone said you left a mean note in
Charlotte's desk.

Ethan: So?

Freddy: Apologize or else!

Ethan: Jeez. Chill. Just a joke.

Freddy: She didn't do it. Tell her you're sorry!!

Between him and Julia:

Julia: She totally lied about my dad.

Freddy: She was super scared.

Julia: Not cool, Freddy!!!!!

Freddy: I know. I'm sorry. She owes you big-time. But
she didn't do it and she's freaking out.

Between him and Chuck:

Chuck: Your sister was in Crenski's office forever!

Freddy: The truth will come out. Give her a chance.

Chuck: My parents heard she had spray paint on her
hands. Doesn't look good.

Freddy: Twins know stuff about each other. I know
she didn't do it.

Freddy turned the phone off.

"Why didn't you show me this stuff right away?" I asked.

"That night I woke you up? Right after it happened? I was a jerk."

"Understatement of the century."

"Anyway, you were so mad. When you're that mad, Charlotte, you're impossible. I thought I'd let it cool down a bit. Then I heard it was Julia's dad, so I figured the whole mess was over. Then I heard it was Bad Chad. I didn't hear it *wasn't* Bad Chad until Mom, Shorty, and me were on the road."

"I guess it all happened pretty fast, but trust me, it didn't feel fast at the time. Every second felt like a year."

"That's how it felt during my first morning alone in school. Two hours took a century. Now I wish it wouldn't go so fast. Before we left Lexington, remember how Mom gave us her standard speech about adventure and making memories and discovering the world?"

"The beautiful journey speech. I could recite it from memory. So is this your beautiful journey?"

"I wouldn't call it a beautiful journey, because I'm not a weirdo," he said. "I want to make some memories that don't stink. That's all."

I thought about the people and places I liked. Julia and Bao. Mia and Miguel. Even Mrs. Newman. I thought about the diner and the gas station and the museum. I thought about the moments that would be my memories.

Playing Truth or Dare. Reading *By the Shores of Silver Lake* in the back seat of our car. Defeating the evil Mrs. Lester in the spelling bee. Tasting gizzard soup.

Freddy said, "Shorty's friend's cousin has a tiny house in town, and he's looking for someone to rent it. I heard him tell Mom about it, and I heard her say she'd like to look at the house. And she applied for a waitressing job."

"Really?"

"Really. So maybe you could figure out a way to like it here, and we could all like it together."

"Maybe," I said. "Maybe I could."

But in my mind I was thinking, *Maybe I already have.*

TWENTY-NINE

Mrs. Newman was back at school the next day, acting as though nothing had happened. The only indication she'd been gone was when she said we were behind on our team science projects, and we'd get extra time. Obviously she knew Mrs. Lester didn't approve of group work or even science.

Then came the moment I'd dreaded: we broke into our science-project teams. I had no idea how people would treat me. Bao and I moved our desks next to the other member of our team, Mihn.

Bao smiled and said hi. Instead of goofing around before we got started, which is what normally happens, Mihn immediately made a list of tasks so we could divide the responsibilities. Freddy's group was all business, too.

My Twin Superpowers sputtered to life and told me Freddy was wondering if his popularity could take another hit—one sister accused of vandalism, the other *guilty* of vandalism. The higher you sit on the social ladder, the more it hurts when you land on your butt.

When Mrs. Newman sent the class to lunch, I stayed behind. She looked up from her desk and said, "Charlotte, you need to have lunch with your classmates."

"I know. I just wanted to tell you that I was sad when you weren't here. And I'm glad that you're here now."

She smiled. "Thank you."

"I'm sorry for what happened to you."

"I did the right thing, so there's no need to apologize. Students shouldn't be cornered without a parent. Let's talk business. Did you read the article about Native Americans?"

"The Trail of Tears article?" My eyes went wide, and I stumbled through an answer, trying to remember what Rose had said about it. "Yes. It was interesting and fascinating. And very sad, too, which is why the word *tears* is in it. Because it's so sad."

She sighed. "Charlotte, you're a terrible liar. I think you should either get better at it or stop entirely. I'd prefer the latter."

"Okay."

"Why? Why haven't you read it?"

I shrugged.

Mrs. Newman sat at her desk. "I will call down to the

lunchroom and ask them to send two trays *if* you attempt to explain it to me."

I nodded and pulled my chair to her desk while she made the call. She hung up and said, "It's chow mein. They probably think it's an authentic Hmong dish." She sighed and stacked the papers on her desk. "All right, I'm listening."

"I don't need to read it to know it's really, really bad. I've read enough about westward expansion."

"Reading and understanding are two different things."

"I know terrible things happened to Native Americans. And terrible things happened to the Chinese with the railroad and poor white farmers in the Depression and all the people fighting over who owned Texas. I'm twelve. I can only take so much sad stuff and guilt before I get Prairie Madness." Mrs. Newman didn't respond, so I said, "I will read it. I promise. But not for a while."

Mrs. Newman thought for a moment. "You have the intellectual capacity to think critically about history. I didn't consider how overwhelming it might be."

"I don't want to hate Laura Ingalls or pioneers or America."

"That's absolutely not my intention. It's just that our country's story is more complicated than most people realize. Laura's story is more complicated."

"I get it," I said. "My story is pretty complicated, too."

"Indeed." She studied me with her serious eyes. "What happens next in your story, Charlotte?"

"I could hardly sleep last night because I was thinking."

I sighed. "I'm going to tell Gloria and Teresa I'm sorry. I should've asked them about what I overheard instead of assuming the worst. I want to go back and finish the online scrapbook."

"That's a good chapter. And after that?"

"I'll try to make it up to Julia and be a better friend, like I won't ever assume bad things about her or her family."

"I like that chapter, too."

"You know, I suppose if I'm trying to correct the negative energy in the universe I would apologize to her dad and to Bad Chad, if he even knows I accused him."

Mrs. Newman nodded. "Your apology will be more effective if you refer to him simply as Chad."

She was full of good ideas, right?

Suddenly I felt tired. "And then there's Mr. Crenski. I should tell him I'm sorry for lying."

"Apologizing to Mr. Crenski? Hmm. Tough one." She wrinkled her nose. "Some apologies are harder than others."

I giggled. Mrs. Newman had a sense of humor.

Who knew?

．．．．．

That night, Mom picked through the refrigerator and reported grim findings. "Three eggs, two cheese sticks, grapes, and sour cream. What's in the cabinet?"

I pulled out a box of macaroni and cheese, but Rose shook her head. "We don't have milk or butter."

"Don't worry about it," Freddy said. "Shorty is bringing frozen pizzas."

Mom glared at him. "Freddy? Did you text Shorty and ask him to bring pizzas?"

"Maybe." He shrugged, but his face broke into a wide grin.

Mom laughed. "I just sent him a text, and he didn't mention a thing about bringing pizzas."

"I asked him to make it a surprise," Freddy said.

"I guess Shorty knows how to keep a secret," I said. "Did you tell him about the Mars book? Because if you did, then we know one hundred percent he can keep a secret. Shorty knows every person in town, and everyone still thinks you're writing the prairie book."

"I told him I'm writing the prairie book, because I am writing the prairie book." She looked down at her shirt. "This shirt is stained. I need to change."

"What do you mean?" Rose asked. "You're not writing about Mars?"

She picked up the toaster and studied her face like it was a mirror. "I need to freshen up."

"Mom!" Freddy took the toaster away. "You're not writing the Mars book?"

"Whenever I open the Mars file, my mind goes blank. My energy drains, and I feel cold and empty and lost. I tried to work on the Mars book every day for six months. Nothing happened. Two weeks ago I opened the prairie file, and the words poured out. I haven't told you, because it feels like a private connection between Laura and me." The door at the top of the stairs opened. Mom whispered, "I'll be in the bathroom cleaning up."

Shorty came down the stairs with two bags of pizzas. Freddy turned on the oven while Rose put glasses and plates on the table. Finally Mom emerged from the bathroom. She'd put on lipstick and tucked her hair into a messy bun.

"Look who's here with pizzas!" Rose beamed.

"And gas station donuts for dessert!" Shorty said.

"What a nice surprise," Mom said.

He pulled packets of hot chocolate out of the bag. "In a few months, we can exchange hot chocolate for lemonade."

Mom's face glowed. "The energy in this town is changing. Spring is coming!"

"Four years ago we had a blizzard in May," Shorty said.

Mom wouldn't let facts get in the way of a good mood. "A spring blizzard will make us appreciate the summer even more."

"We'll definitely appreciate June if it snows in May," Rose said. "June will seem perfect."

You saw that coming, right?

ALL'S WELL THAT ENDS WELL

The snowmelt and spring rains caused Plum Creek to swell and spill over its banks. Even though it was May, winter hadn't released its grip on the prairie. Some kids in our class were already wearing shorts, but we shivered in our light jackets.

It was Freddy's first trip to the dugout. We'd come to get a short video for the online scrapbook, but we also had a personal mission.

"Check out the creek," Freddy said. "It even sounds flooded. I'm sure I could hear it with my hearing aids off. The video idea is genius. People can imagine the Ingallses living right next to this rushing river."

"The video was Julia's idea," I said.

Julia had decided to give me another chance, mostly because she needed advice about Freddy, who'd started walking home with Lanie Erickson. I kept my promise to Julia. I didn't share her secrets with anybody, especially Freddy.

Freddy walked to the sign near the Ingallses' former dugout and read it. "THE CHARLES INGALLS FAMILY'S DUGOUT HOME WAS LOCATED HERE IN THE 1870S. THIS DEPRESSION IS ALL THAT REMAINS SINCE THE ROOF CAVED IN YEARS AGO. THE PRAIRIE GRASSES AND FLOWERS HERE GROW MUCH AS THEY DID IN LAURA'S TIME AND THE SPRING STILL FLOWS NEARBY." He shook his head. "I still can't believe people lived in a dirt hole. That's bananas."

"Mom thought about putting a dugout in her book, but she decided that was too much like Laura's story," I said.

"I like the Mars idea better."

"Rose told me the prairie book is good. Mom read the first couple of chapters to her when we were at Noah's party. Wouldn't it be awesome if she sold it and could write full-time? Because her waitressing career isn't promising."

Freddy raised his eyebrow. "Evidence?"

"Yesterday she spilled a glass of milk on a customer."

He laughed. "She's getting better."

"Evidence?"

"Shorty says Mom gets decent tips because of her sunny personality," he said. "I know it could all change in a few weeks. We might end up in Utah. But it's good for now, right?"

"Utah? Do you have evidence?" I couldn't hide the worry in my voice.

"No new evidence," he said. "Just history."

We approached the walking bridge where Rose was standing. She peered over the rail, watching the creek as it cut through the same swath of land it had followed for centuries. Mom and Shorty crossed from the other bank holding hands. I worried that Mom would discover Shorty wasn't the man she thought he was, that he'd end up on the bad-husband list along with our dad and Rey. But Mia assured me he was a good guy. She said Shorty's brother's mother-in-law had told her Shorty was crazy about Mom.

We gathered around Rose as she opened the Jack bag and took out the box of ashes. "This creek is thirty-five miles long. I did my research," she said. "It flows into the Cottonwood River, which flows into the Minnesota River, which flows into the Mississippi River, which empties into the Gulf of Mexico."

"That's quite a journey for our Jack," Mom said. "I think it's beautiful."

"I can't do it. You do it." Rose handed the box to me.

"You can, and you should," I said. "He'd want it to be you."

Rose thought for a minute and then nodded. She gave

the box one final squeeze. "Good-bye, Jack," she said. "We miss you." Then Rose removed the top and poured Jack's remains into Laura's creek.

The ashes settled on the surface and, in a second, they were gone.

· ACKNOWLEDGMENTS ·

Charlotte's story began during a writing retreat with my friends Stephanie and Michelle at a beautiful lake home provided by Kristi and Mike. I can't thank them enough for their hospitality.

On that retreat, I took notes for Charlotte's story, but I also read several books about Laura's life. The most influential of those books were *Laura Ingalls Wilder: A Biography* by William Anderson, *Pioneer Girl* by Laura Ingalls Wilder (annotated by Pamela Smith Hill), and *Laura Ingalls Wilder: A Writer's Life* by Pamela Smith Hill. I'm grateful to William Anderson and Pamela Smith Hill for their expertise. I highly recommend their books to Laura fans.